AMELIA FANG

AND THE BARBARIC BALL

Also by

LAURA ELLEN ANDERSON

AMELIA FANG

AND THE UNICORNS
OF GLITTEROPOLIS

AMELIA FANG

AND THE BARBARIC BALL

LAURA ELLEN ANDERSON

DELACORTE PRESS

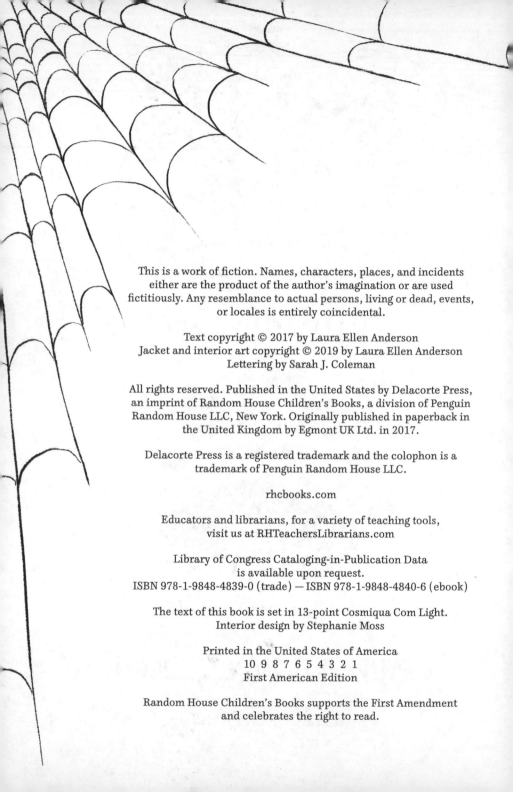

Text copyright © 2017 by Laura Ellen Anderson
Jacket and interior art copyright © 2019 by Laura Ellen Anderson
Lettering by Sarah J. Coleman

rhcbooks.com

Educators and librarians, for a variety of teaching tools, visit us at RHTeachersLibrarians.com

Library of Congress Cataloging-in-Publication Data is available upon request.
ISBN 978-1-9848-4839-0 (trade) — ISBN 978-1-9848-4840-6 (ebook)

The text of this book is set in 13-point Cosmiqua Com Light.
Interior design by Stephanie Moss

Printed in the United States of America
10 9 8 7 6 5 4 3 2 1
First American Edition

For Helen

*Thank you for believing in Amelia and supplying me
with unicorn-shaped inspiration and surprise loose limbs!
Your continued support, encouragement
and enthusiasm won't be forgotten.*

*And a special THANKS to all the FANG-GIRLS.
You know who you are!*

x Yeti hugs x

CONTENTS

Ghoulish Greetings
from our favorite
Nocturnians . . .

SQUASHY

AMELIA FANG

LIKES:
Bouncing
Hugs

DISLIKES:
Being picked up by his stem
Not being with Amelia

LIKES:
Squashy (her loyal pet pumpkin)
Tongue Twister Sandwiches

DISLIKES:
Spoiled sprouts
The annual Barbaric Ball

GRIMALDI REAPERTON

FLORENCE SPUDWICK

LIKES:
Pit digging
Worms on toast

DISLIKES:
Being called a BEAST
(She is a RARE BREED
OF YETI.)

LIKES:
His scythe
His diePhone

DISLIKES:
Bossy squished toads
Unicorns

COUNTESS FRIVOLEETA

COUNT DRAKE THE THIRD

LIKES:
Crosswords
His Hawaiian graveyard
shirts

DISLIKES:
Washing up
Listening

LIKES:
The annual Barbaric Ball
Eau de Decay perfume

DISLIKES:
Her husband's Hawaiian
graveyard shirts
Goblin slime

LIKES:
Cooking
Letter writing

DISLIKES:
Bad manners
Being walked through

WOOO

OVER 10,000 CROSSWORD PUZZLES

CHAPTER 1

FLABBERGASTING FETTUCCINE

It was a dark and gloomy Wednesday night in Nocturnia. Countess Frivoleeta Fang sipped her Scream Tea and tapped the dining-room table with her long black fingernails as the clock struck four a.m.

"Drake, my darkness, you do know it's our annual Barbaric Ball in just three nights?" Countess Frivoleeta cooed. "We still have invitations to send, catering to sort out and— oh, did you book the Howling Wolf Band?"

Count Drake's eyes widened. "Erm . . . I'll phone them tonight, dearest rat brains."

"And, Drakey, you'll need to wear your best suit for the ball. None of those

Hawaiian graveyard shirts you like so much. We really must find a way to unstick all that goblin slime from last year's ball too . . ."

(Goblins were notorious for leaving slime trails—stickier than the stickiest super glue, they were impossible to remove!)

"Not another Barbaric Ball," moaned Amelia Fang, slumping back into her chair. "They're always full of old monsters wearing too many frills and far too much Eau de Decay."

Amelia had just turned ten and would rather hang out with her best friends, Florence and Grimaldi, than go to the ball.

"Amelia Fang! I won't have any of that bat-chat from you," the countess said sternly. "Firstly, Eau de Decay is the finest perfume in all of Nocturnia. It's made from fermented bat spit with a hint of rotten banana, after all! And secondly, the Barbaric Ball is a family tradition. It's our chance to show everyone how fang-tastic we are."

Amelia knew this already. The Fang family had hosted the Barbaric Ball for generations. It was THE annual event in Nocturnia. Only the most ghoulish and ghastly were invited, and the ball was Countess Frivoleeta's pride and joy.

"But I get so bored," Amelia grumbled. "It would be much better if someone my own age were there!"

"You know the ball is only for grown-ups," the countess said.

"Then surely I don't have

to go?" Amelia said hopefully.

"Of *course* you have to go. You must learn the ropes so that you can carry on the Barbaric Ball tradition!" her mother said with a gleeful grin.

"But what if I don't want to?" Amelia mumbled. "I want to study pumpkinology when I grow up, and help sick pumpkins."

Countess Frivoleeta burst out laughing.

"Darkling! Don't be silly. Oh, you'll make my eye makeup run!" She checked her face in the mirror behind her, then blew herself a kiss. (You may have heard that vampires don't have reflections. That is false, and no one loved theirs more than Countess Frivoleeta.) "You'd ruin your delicate vampiress hands with all the digging. Now sit up straight for dinner," she continued. "Wooo!"

Amelia sighed as a ghost floated into the room, carrying a tray of something that looked like a pile of big boogies.

It was useless for Amelia to try to speak to her mother about what *she* wanted. Being a Fang meant countless vampiress etiquette lessons, cobwebbing practice and never-ending preparations for the Barbaric Ball. Sometimes Amelia wished she belonged to a different family.

"Your Flabbergasting Fettuccine, Countess," said Wooo. He was the most respected ghost butler in all of Nocturnia.

(Contrary to popular belief, vampires don't actually live on a diet of blood. It gives them very stinky breath!)

"Thank you, Wooo. That will be all," the countess said.

Amelia flapped her wings grumpily and flicked a piece of fettuccine onto the floor.

Her pet pumpkin, Squashy, gobbled it up, then bounced onto Amelia's lap.

"Hey, Squashy!" Amelia giggled. "Have some more fettuccine! I know it's your favorite."

Squashy wiggled his stem from side to side in agreement.

"Maybe the king will come to the ball this year?" Amelia said through a mouthful of sour spinach.

"Not likely," Countess Frivoleeta said. "He hasn't stepped outside the palace since *the fairy incident*." She looked at her husband. "Drakey, my awful little germinoid, you should really make more of an effort to see King Vladimir. You two used to be such good friends."

Count Drake gave a long sigh. "Dearest belch-breath, it's no use. He won't see or speak to anyone anymore."

"Such a shame," Countess Frivoleeta said.

"Ever since he canceled your weekly Eyebowls game, you've been completely obsessed with those silly word-crosses. . . ."

"Crosswords, dear," Count Drake said.

"If the king DID accept our invitation to the ball, do you think he would bring his son?" Amelia asked. Her eyes lit up for a moment. "Or is Prince Tangine not allowed to come either, because he's not *old*?"

"Prince Tangine is the future king, for serpent's sake! He is ALWAYS invited," the countess sang.

"But remember, Amelia," Count Drake added, "the prince's mother DID get eaten by a fairy. I'd be surprised if the king ever lets him outside the palace walls."

"Grieving goblins, I'd go mad if I couldn't go and see my friends," Amelia said.

"Enough chitchat. Now, Amelia, eat up before your fettuccine gets cold, then off to

bed," Countess Frivoleeta said, prodding at her daughter's cheeks. "We must keep your skin looking pale and deathlike!"

"But, Mooom, it's the final of *The Great Gothic Gravestone Carve-Off* tonight! Can't I stay up for just a bit longer?" Amelia said.

Suddenly, a huge BOOOOOOONG! echoed through the house.

"Drake, my little sweat gland, are we expecting visitors?" Countess Frivoleeta said. "Wooo!" she called without waiting for her husband's reply. "Please answer that immediately."

Moments later, Wooo appeared holding a gold envelope.

"You have a letter, Countess. It appears to be from the king."

CHAPTER 2

FLORENCE
AND GRIMALDI

"THE KING'S COMING TO THE BALL?"
Florence yelled. This was normal speaking
volume for Florence, who was six feet tall,
huge and hairy from head to toe. Everything
about her was BIG. Even her voice was big.
But so was her heart. Which was also very
hairy. She was Amelia's best friend.

Amelia, Squashy and Florence Spudwick
were sitting under the Petrified-Tree-That-
Looked-Like-a-Unicorn, where they met
every night before school.

"THAT'S SO EXCITING!" roared Florence, gobbling down a bowl of Unlucky Arms cereal.

"And he's bringing the prince!" Amelia said excitedly. "I'll finally have someone my OWN age to hang out with at the ball! Although I still wish you and Grimaldi could come."

"S'ALL RIGHT," said Florence, putting a hairy arm around Amelia's shoulders. "I'D SHOW EVERYONE UP WITH MY STUNNING LOOKS!" She grinned, revealing a mouthful of spiky teeth pointing in every direction.

The two friends burst out laughing.

Squashy bounced up and down, blowing raspberries with his tongue, before nuzzling into Amelia's tummy for a belly rub.

"Hi, guuuuys!" came a high voice from across the graveyard. It was Grimaldi Reaperton, Amelia's other best friend.

Grimaldi was small and cute, and Death

was his middle name. (No, really, it was. He dealt with the deaths of small creatures, like squished toads, but when he was older, he would take over from his grimpapa and deal with bigger, messier beings.)

"Grimaldi!" Amelia said excitedly. "I have BIG news!"

"Is it about *The Great Gothic Gravestone Carve-Off*?" Grimaldi said. "Because I really thought that William W—"

"Whoa, whoa, whoa! Don't tell me. I haven't seen the final episode yet . . . ," said Amelia, covering her ears.

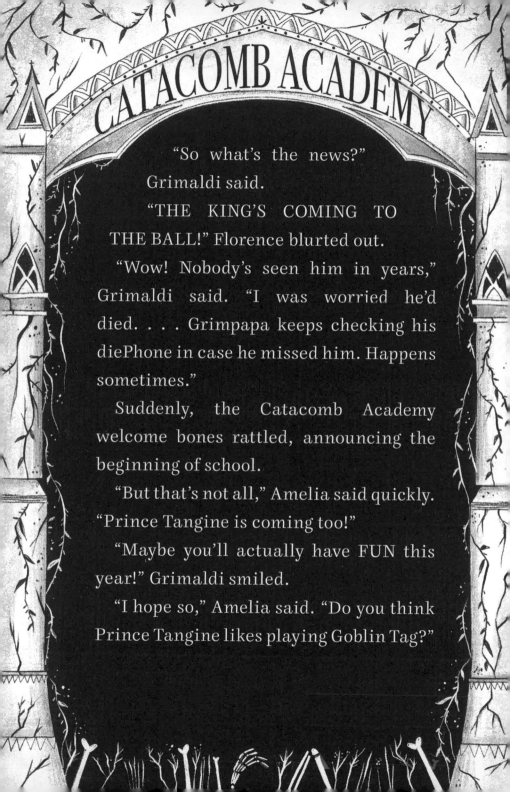

"So what's the news?" Grimaldi said.

"THE KING'S COMING TO THE BALL!" Florence blurted out.

"Wow! Nobody's seen him in years," Grimaldi said. "I was worried he'd died. . . . Grimpapa keeps checking his diePhone in case he missed him. Happens sometimes."

Suddenly, the Catacomb Academy welcome bones rattled, announcing the beginning of school.

"But that's not all," Amelia said quickly. "Prince Tangine is coming too!"

"Maybe you'll actually have FUN this year!" Grimaldi smiled.

"I hope so," Amelia said. "Do you think Prince Tangine likes playing Goblin Tag?"

"Amelia!" Miss Inspine
shouted. She was the
head teacher. "Florence,
Grimaldi! Hurry up!
You're going to be late for
Abominable Assembly!"

Amelia and her
friends wound their
way down to the Catacomb
Academy crypt.

"Whose lap do you want
to sit on today, Squashy?"
Amelia asked.

Squashy immediately
pa-doinged into
Amelia's arms and
started licking her face.

"I think that's settled!" she
said, laughing.

In the crypt, the music

teacher, Mr. Blob, was playing the "Death March" on the organ. Then he exploded, his way of saying the assembly was about to begin. An eyeball landed in the hood of Grimaldi's cloak.

"EVERY time!" Grimaldi grimaced.

"Okay, class, take your seats, please," Miss Inspine said. "First, I'd like to make a very special announcement. As you all know, the Barbaric Ball is taking place in a couple of nights. And I'm happy to announce that King Vladimir will be attending with his son, Prince Tangine, after all these years!"

The students buzzed excitedly.

"I have ALSO been informed that, as of tonight, Prince Tangine will be joining Catacomb Academy as part of his king training, to get to know the young creatures of Nocturnia!"

The whole crypt exploded in squeals and burps of delight.

"Oh, isn't it just AWFUL that his mother was EATEN by a fairy?" cried Frankie. She had stitches over her face and bolts in her neck.

"There will be NO mention of *the fairy incident*," Miss Inspine hissed. "The prince is probably anxious enough, leaving the palace for the first time in years."

"So brave!" said Frankie, fanning herself with her detached ear.

"The king has requested," the head teacher continued, "that Amelia Fang show Prince Tangine around the school and look after him while he settles in."

"That's only because the king used to be best buddies with Amelia's dad!" Frankie spat.

Amelia muffled a groan. Frankie was the most annoying ghoul in Catacomb Academy.

"Enough, Frankie!" said Miss Inspine, losing patience. "The prince is due to arrive any minute, and I want you ALL to be on your BEST behavior."

"Imagine." Grimaldi grinned. "The three of us hanging out with the future king! We'll be the coolest kids in school."

"HEY," Florence said. "WE ALREADY ARE."

I wonder what Tangine is like, Amelia thought, when a loud noise caught her attention.

SQUAAAAAWK! **CRASH!**

"You stupid bird! Why can't you ever land properly?" came a high-pitched voice.

"Oh! Wait here, everyone. . . ." Miss Inspine said, scampering out of the crypt.

Seconds later she returned looking flustered.

"Students! It gives me great pleasure to welcome our special new student to Catacomb Academy . . . Prince Tangine!"

CHAPTER 3

TANGINE

A long shadow appeared, stretching the length of the crypt. Amelia watched as the shadow became smaller, and smaller . . . and smaller . . .

Until Prince Tangine stepped into view.

"HOW WEENY IS HE?" Florence whispered loudly.

Miss Inspine shot her a sharp look.

The prince was tiny. Teeny, even. Which was very unusual for a vampire.

Frankie began applauding frantically. "Tangine rules! Tangine, you're amazing!" she yelled across the room.

"JOSEPHINE!" shouted Tangine, clapping his tiny hands twice.

A Mummy Maid ran in and crouched at Tangine's feet so he could use her as a platform.

"Yes, it is I, your future king!" said Prince Tangine, revealing his pearly white fangs. "I suppose I look forward to learning stuff at your *little* school."

Amelia was surprised by Prince Tangine's

tone. *He must be nervous,* she thought.

"Anyway," continued Tangine, yawning. "I'm bored. I demand brunch. . . ." He clapped his hands again and shouted, "FRESCO!"

Maybe he gets hungry when he's nervous, Amelia thought.

Another Mummy Maid rushed into the crypt, holding a tray of Slug-Ends.

"Ooh, isn't he delightful?" Frankie oozed as the Mummy Maid crawled back out of the crypt, still carrying Tangine.

"Well." Amelia looked at Florence and Grimaldi. "Tangine seems . . . nice?"

After Abominable Assembly, Amelia waited outside Miss Inspine's room for Prince Tangine. He was already ten minutes late for class. *Maybe he's lost?* she thought.

Squashy sniffed around inside Amelia's backpack, looking for something to chew.

"No, no, Squashy, that's my homework!" Amelia giggled. "I knew you'd get hungry, so I took some of Dad's breakfast for you. . . ."

Amelia pulled out a fistful of Honey-Roasted Maggots, and Squashy gently nibbled them from her hand.

She was still feeding him and rubbing his pumpkin tummy when a voice echoed down the corridor.

"Aren't you going to show me to the classroom?"

"Oh!" said Amelia, jumping to her feet. Tangine was standing proudly on a Mummy Maid at the end of the corridor. "Hello, Prince Tangine!" She smiled.

"INGRID. Crawl!" the prince demanded.

"It's so good to finally meet you," said Amelia. "Our fathers used to play Eyebowls

together every week, y'know. Maybe we could ask them to teach us?"

Tangine didn't answer.

"And it's really cool that you're coming to the Barbaric Ball!" she went on. "I usually hate going on my own. My mom makes me dance with all the posh old toads!"

Silence.

"At least I'll have someone to hang out with this year. . . ."

"What's that?" Tangine said suddenly, pointing at Squashy.

"Oh, this is Squashy, my pet pumpkin," Amelia said.

Squashy smiled and squeaked three times.

"Pets are silly," said Tangine, rolling his eyes.

Amelia's cheeks burned. "Um . . . ," she started uncomfortably. "Well, should we go to class?"

"Don't they teach you manners in this school?" Tangine said. "I am royalty. You must open the door for me!"

Amelia felt herself blush again, but then the door suddenly burst open.

"Oh, thank the grave!" Miss Inspine sighed. "I thought you'd lost the prince, Amelia. Chop-chop, you've made him late for class!"

"But, Miss, I—" Amelia began.

"Not now, Amelia," the head teacher said. "Hurry up. There's a special seat for Tangine next to you."

THE WRATH OF
The Angel-Kitten
By Dr. Alfaewny Kawn

CHAPTER 4
ANGEL-KITTENS OF TERROR

Amelia and Tangine took their seats while Squashy nestled under the desk.

"Did everyone complete their Creature and Critter Studies homework?" Miss Inspine said. "Your Full Moon test is coming up, and this year's subject is Creatures of the Light. Can anyone tell me what they've learned so far?"

"Oooh, me, me, me, pick me!" Frankie shot her hand up in the air.

"Very well." Miss Inspine sighed.

Frankie stood up and cleared her throat. "Well, we all know that the Creatures of the

Light are terrifying, mean creatures who do awful things. . . ."

"This is a stupid subject," Tangine muttered.

"I read a book called *The Wrath of the Angel-Kitten*," Frankie continued, "and they act all cute and nuzzle your neck but then they scratch your eyeballs out and eat them WHOLE!"

The class gasped. Tangine was looking down, twiddling his thumbs.

"Thank you for that dramatic account, Frankie," Miss Inspine said with another deep sigh.

"And we all know that fairies are capable of MUCH worse." Frankie glanced over at Tangine. "I'm soooo sorry about your mother—"

"That is enough, Frankie!" Miss Inspine interrupted. "I told you not to mention

the fairy incident!" she hissed.

"Can't we learn about something else?" Tangine said sharply, straightening up in his chair.

It must be hard for him after what happened to his mother, Amelia thought.

Amelia and her friends loved reading stories about the Creatures of the Light: the gruesome glittery unicorns (Nocturnians were TERRIFIED of glitter), the evil sparkly fairies and the cute and fluffy angel-kittens of terror. (Everyone knew that while Nocturnians were sleeping and the sun was out, terrifying creatures from the nearby Kingdom of the Light lurked around the Petrified Forest. Nocturnians didn't dare step outside again until nightfall, if they could help it.)

"Florence," Miss Inspine trilled, "did you do any research on the subject?"

"MATTER OF FACT, I DID . . . ," Florence said, standing up. "MY MOM READ ME A BOOK CALLED *FEARFUL FACTS ABOUT FRIGHTFUL FAIRIES*. THEY USE THAT SPARKLY STUFF CALLED GLITTER AND SPRINKLE IT ALL OVER YOU, MAKING YOU FALL INTO A DEEP SLEEP. THEN . . ." She paused. "WHILE YOU'RE SLEEPING SOUNDLY, THEY USE THEIR LITTLE WANDS TO . . ." She leaned forward, staring at Frankie intensely. "STEAL YOUR FANGS!"

Grimaldi yelped and pulled his hood over his face. Amelia put her hand over her mouth.

"Oh, don't be so over-the-top, Beast!" said Tangine.

Amelia, Florence and Grimaldi stared at the prince in shock.

"WHAT DID YOU JUST CALL ME?" said Florence, rising up to her full height.

"Well, that's what you are, isn't it? A

beast who doesn't shut up?" said Tangine, avoiding eye contact.

"Hey! That's a really mean thing to say," Amelia said. She couldn't believe the prince had called Florence a beast. There was no excuse for that, even if he was nervous.

Florence loomed over Tangine. "I AM NOT A BEAST!" she boomed. "I'M A RARE BREED OF YETI!"

"Florence Spudwick!" shouted Miss Inspine, causing her ribs to rattle. "Leave the prince alone and sit down this instant!"

"BUT, MISS, HE CALLED ME A—"

"Now!" said Miss Inspine. "Right. Please open your books to page thirty-two and answer the questions on angel-kitten history. You have fifteen minutes." And with that, she took off her head and put it in the cupboard for some peace and quiet.

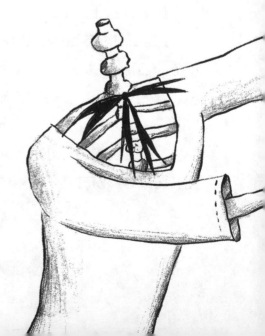

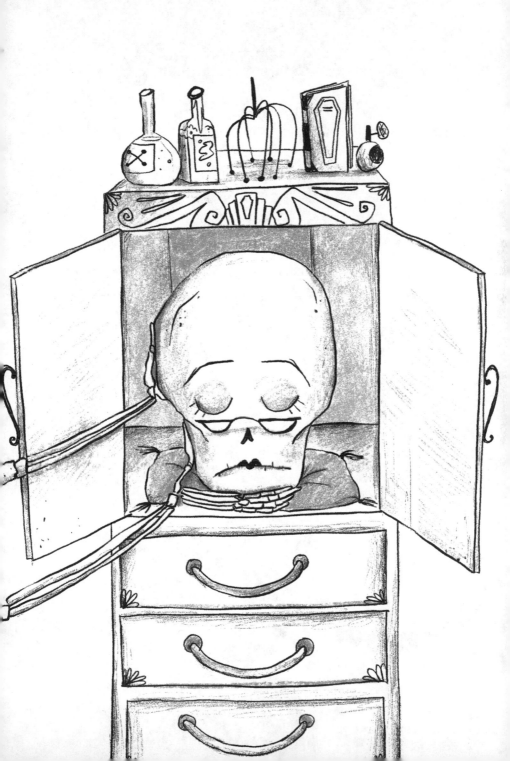

CHAPTER 5

YOU AAAAAARE DEAD, YOU ARE DEAD

At the end of the school night, Amelia walked Tangine to the academy entrance in silence. Florence and Grimaldi followed, keeping their distance.

Amelia still couldn't believe Tangine had been so mean to Florence. The prince wasn't like she'd imagined he'd be at all. But maybe he would be better tomorrow. "Um . . . is your dad picking you up from school?" Amelia finally said.

"No. John will be taking me home," said

Tangine, pointing to a huge vulture whose three eyes all looked in different directions.

"Oh. Well, it was, um, nice to meet you," said Amelia, looking at her feet. "See you tomorrow, I guess."

"You'll be seeing me tonight, actually," Tangine sneered. "Your mother practically begged Father and me to come to your house for a pre–Barbaric Ball dinner."

Amelia wasn't sure what to say. "Oh . . . great!" she spluttered.

Once Tangine was out of sight, Amelia, Florence and Grimaldi each let out a big sigh of relief.

"WELL, HE'S HORRIBLE," said Florence. "AND NOT IN THE NICE WAY."

"I'm sorry he called you names, Florence," Amelia said. "At first I thought he was nervous, starting a new school and all, but that's no excuse for being so mean."

Suddenly, Grimaldi's diePhone rang out:

YOU AAAAAARE DEAD, YOU ARE DEAD,
FROM THE TIPS OF YOUR TOES TO THE TOP
OF YOUR HEAD. . . .

"WHO DIED?" asked Florence.

"Hmmm. It's your mom," said Grimaldi, looking at Amelia.

"WHAT?" Florence gasped.

"No, no, no. Amelia's mom is *calling* me. . . ." Grimaldi answered the phone. "Um, hello, Mrs. Fang. Sorry, I mean, Mrs. Fountess Cang. Wait, I mean, Countess Fang . . ."

Amelia took the phone from Grimaldi, who was now blushing and biting his nails. "Hey, Mom," she said.

"Amelia, you must come home this instant," Countess Frivoleeta said, sounding out of breath. "King Vladimir and Prince Tangine are coming for dinner!"

"I heard," said Amelia. "But can't I stay out

with Florence and Grimaldi for a little while? I won't be late for dinner, I promise."

"We need to make the house look PERFECT. You must come home now, Amelia!" insisted the countess, and then hung up the phone.

YOU AAAAAARE DEAD, YOU ARE DEAD, FROM THE TIPS OF YOUR TOES TO THE TOP OF YOUR HEAD . . . chimed the diePhone again.

"What could my mother possibly want now?" Amelia said.

"It's a real death this time. . . . Two squished toads." Grimaldi sighed. "Sorry, guys. Gotta go."

"LOOKS LIKE WE WON'T BE HANGING OUT TONIGHT, THEN," said Florence.

"I'm afraid not," Amelia said, stroking Squashy. "Sorry."

"Okay," Florence said. She turned to Grimaldi. "LEMME KNOW IF ANY OF

THOSE SQUISHED TOADS DON'T WANT THEIR KIDNEYS. I CAN USE 'EM FOR MY ART PROJECT."

"Sure thing," Grimaldi said, chuckling as he disappeared into the mist.

Amelia and Florence wandered through Central Nocturnia Graveyard while Squashy bounced his way across the gravestones.

"I wonder what the king looks like now," Amelia said. "I've seen pictures in books, and my mom's always saying how he's more handsome than my dad. . . ."

"DUNNO," Florence said. "IMAGINE IF HE HAD A BIG PIMPLE ON HIS NOSE. . . ."

Amelia giggled. "What do you mean?"

"WELL, PEOPLE THINK ROYALTY ARE ALL PERFECT. BUT I BET THEY GET PIMPLES ON THEIR NOSES TOO. AND THEIR BUTTS."

Amelia laughed so hard she snorted.

"MY GRANNY DORIS HAD ONE ON HER BUTT CHEEK FOR SEVENTY YEARS," Florence said thoughtfully.

"Well, I'd better get home," Amelia said with a sigh. "Maybe Tangine will be nicer in a smaller group. . . ."

"IF HE'S MEAN TO YOU, JUST LEMME KNOW AND I'LL COME AND SIT ON HIM."

Amelia smiled and hugged her friend. "Thanks, Florence. What would I do without you?"

"PROBABLY BE VERY BORED," Florence replied, laughing.

CHAPTER 6
THE TOILET ISN'T SHINY ENOUGH

When Amelia arrived home, Countess Frivoleeta seemed rather flustered.

"There's so much to do! Wooo, is the toilet shiny? IT HAS TO BE SHINY!" she shrieked, making Squashy bounce into Amelia's arms. Sometimes Amelia wished her parents were a little less ridiculous.

"I can't believe the king is coming to dinner. This is HUGE! The first time in YEARS!" Countess Frivoleeta's left eyeball popped out in her excitement. "We must make sure everything is PERFECT! Amelia, get changed into something . . . blacker," she said, dusting her eyeball and popping it back in.

"I'm already wearing all black," said Amelia, wrinkling her nose.

"Well. Something even MORE black . . . with more frills!" the countess added before disappearing through a door.

Count Drake shuffled into the hall in his fluffy slippers.

"Aren't you helping?" asked Amelia.

"Me?" her father said, stretching up his arms and revealing his potbelly. "I've helped loads. I took my mug . . ." He paused and smiled. "And I put it . . ." He looked serious. "In the sink."

Amelia was impressed. That was more cleaning than he'd ever done. Ever.

"And look! I've only got two clues left in my crossword," he said, flapping the *Midnight Times* at Amelia.

"Oh, Squashy," said Amelia, hugging him to her chest. "Mom and Dad have really lost it this time!"

BOOOOOOOOOONG! went the door gong.

"THEY'RE EARLY!" Countess Frivoleeta screeched from the second floor. "I haven't CHANGED . . . and the TOILET isn't SHINY enough! Wooo, distract them while I polish my fangs!"

Amelia ran up the stairs, with Squashy following close behind, and perched on the first-floor balcony, just out of sight.

Adjusting his monocle, Wooo opened the front door.

"Welcome to the Fang residence. My name is Wooo," he said, and gave a graceful bow.

"Yes, yes, thank you," came a deep, shaky voice.

"Please, come in," Wooo said, gesturing

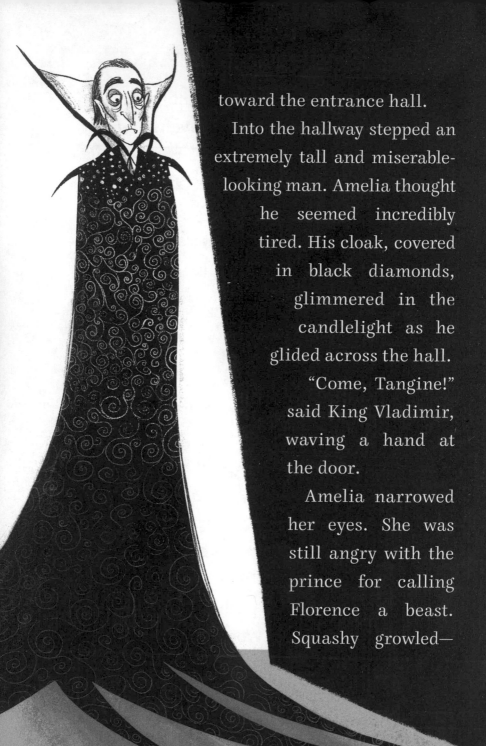

toward the entrance hall.

Into the hallway stepped an extremely tall and miserable-looking man. Amelia thought he seemed incredibly tired. His cloak, covered in black diamonds, glimmered in the candlelight as he glided across the hall.

"Come, Tangine!" said King Vladimir, waving a hand at the door.

Amelia narrowed her eyes. She was still angry with the prince for calling Florence a beast. Squashy growled—

although it sounded more like a cute gurgle.

Tangine stepped into the hall, putting his hands on his hips. "Hmmm, I thought our home was cramped, and we have over three thousand rooms," he said casually. "But this place is like a cupboard."

Amelia frowned. He was still acting like a spoiled sprout.

"The count and countess will be with you shortly," Wooo said. "Can I get you anything to drink? We have homemade Eyeball Juice or Armpit-Sweat Shakes?"

"I'll take a Sweat Shake, please," the king mumbled.

"Make that two!" said Tangine. "Thanks, Ooo."

"It's Wooo, sir," said Wooo.

"Oh, forgive me, Woe," said Tangine, not even looking at Wooo. He was busy wiping one of his shoes on the carpet. "Hmmm, I think I stepped on something outside. It just won't . . ." He scraped his foot harder. "Come . . ." Then he kicked really hard.

"OFF!"

A piece of glittery goop flew off his shoe and straight through Wooo. At the same moment, Countess Frivoleeta burst through a door, wearing her brand-new dress.

SPLAT!

The glitter goop landed on Countess Frivoleeta's chest.

Just then, Count Drake entered the hall in his gloomiest Hawaiian graveyard shirt.

"VLADIMIR!" He beamed, putting an arm around the king's shoulders. "It has been too long, my friend. You're looking . . . gaunt." He patted the king. "Perhaps you could come and help me with my latest crossword while we wait for din—" Suddenly, he stopped dead, staring at the countess's dress. His hands began to shake. "Oooh, my . . . ," he said, gasping. "Is that g-g-g-g-glitter?"

CHAPTER 7

DO SOMETHING, DADDY!

Countess Frivoleeta looked as if she might burst into tears as the big sticky glob of glitter slipped its way down her dress. But, to Amelia's surprise, her mother paused, gulped and then gave a shaky smile.

"Oooh, it's o-o-o-kay." She laughed brightly, even though Amelia knew she was just as afraid as Amelia herself was. "A bit of g-g-gl-aaaaah . . . won't hurt!"

Countess Frivoleeta floated past Tangine and curtseyed, wobbling slightly as the glitter goop reached her knee.

"King Vladimir," she gushed, "it is an honor to have you here in our home after so long. And we are DELIGHTED you can come to the ball this year!"

"Yes, yes, pleasure," said the king, turning away from the countess. He didn't seem at all bothered by the glitter pooling on the floor.

"And this is Tangine," the king said.

Tangine raised his eyebrows and grinned.

"Well, aren't you just repugnant!" Countess Frivoleeta said in a high-pitched voice.

"Amelia, darkling, where are you? Come down here this instant and say hello to our guests!"

"Where are those manners, Miss

Ameeelia?" Tangine said. "Probably been spending too much time hanging around with that beastly friend of yours!"

Before Amelia could say anything, Squashy pa-doinged his way down the stairs and bit the prince's nose.

"OOOOOOOW!" Tangine shrieked. "OOOH, DADDY! Do something, Daddy!"

Countess Frivoleeta was so shocked, one of her eyebrows fell off and ran away. Amelia raced down the stairs to scoop up Squashy.

"Oh, my wobbly werewolves, I'm SO sorry! Please forgive him. He's just overexcited!" the countess said.

"Aren't you going to say something, Daddy?" Tangine moaned.

"Oh, you'll be fine," King Vladimir said half-heartedly.

Amelia watched King Vladimir's blank

face. He didn't seem to care very much about anything, including his own son.

"Daddy," said Tangine, luckily getting distracted by a statue that stood next to the front door. "We don't have a statue of Lord Ey-Ey Pistachio the Eighth in our palace."

"No, we don't," the king agreed.

"We've had that statue of the founder of Nocturnia in our family for generations," the countess said proudly.

"I want one," said Tangine, pouting at his father.

"Very well. I'll get you one," the king said.

"No. I want *that* one," said Tangine, pointing at the small statue.

Countess Frivoleeta made a soft choking sound. "Oh, I—I—I don't think—"

"Fine," interrupted King Vladimir, picking up the statue.

Countess Frivoleeta glanced over at

Count Drake, but he was busy studying his crossword puzzle.

"I guess that's . . . okay. Consider it a . . . welcome-back gift," Countess Frivoleeta said in a small voice.

"There," said the king, handing the statue to Tangine without a blink.

"Now, where's that ghost WooWoo with our Sweat Shakes?" Tangine demanded.

Countess Frivoleeta's makeup was starting to run.

"Amelia," she hissed, "take the prince to the bathroom and find some Crispy Carcass Cream for his poor nose."

"Mooom," Amelia groaned. "I don't want—"

"Now!" Countess Frivoleeta snapped.

Luckily, at that moment, Wooo arrived with the drinks.

"Apologies for the delay," he announced. "We always make the Armpit-Sweat Shakes from scratch."

The king grabbed a tall glass with a thin, trembling hand. Tangine drank his whole shake in one gulp, then belched loudly.

"Too salty," he said, throwing the glass back onto the tray.

"I think I'll just change into some clean clothes before dinner is served. This was, erm, just my welcome dress," said Countess Frivoleeta, glancing at the glittery stain and shuddering.

"Well?" said Tangine, turning to Amelia. "Where's the bathroom?"

Amelia stomped up the stairs, while Squashy gave Tangine his most menacing

stare, which still
looked pretty cute.

"Does that pumpkin
go everywhere with
you?" Tangine said as
they wound their way up
the spiral staircase.

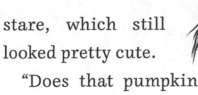

Amelia spun
around. "Squashy is
the nicest pumpkin ever.
He only bites if somebody is
being really mean!"

Tangine began twiddling his
thumbs. "Look at all these doors,"
he said, ignoring Amelia. "I like
this one. . . ." He was about to

touch a big black door covered with intricate silver decorations, but it burst into flames.

"What was THAT?" squealed Tangine, falling backward.

"The doors do that sometimes," Amelia said, unable to contain her grin.

"How dare they?" Tangine said. "And why are there so many doors in this house? It's far too small to have this many rooms."

"They're not all rooms," Amelia said mysteriously.

In fact, there were doors of all shapes and sizes lining every corridor of the Fang house. Some doors led to rooms on different floors and some led outside the mansion, while others simply disappeared one day, never to be seen again.

Amelia opened a big red door into complete darkness. "Anyway, here's the bathroom...." she said.

"That's not a bathroom," Tangine said. "There's nothing in there."

Amelia rolled her eyes. "Just go in. It'll take you to the bathroom, you'll see."

"No," said Tangine, folding his arms. "What if it bursts into flames when I walk in? You have to come in with me."

"I'm NOT going to the bathroom with you," Amelia said.

Tangine's cheeks flushed. "DAAAADDYYYYYY!" he called.

"Oh, fine!" Amelia said quickly. "Stop being so silly!"

Tangine followed Amelia through the red door. The next thing they knew, they were in a HUGE room with a tiny toilet and a sink in the center. The room was so big that Amelia's and Tangine's voices echoed.

"Hmmm," Tangine said thoughtfully. "That toilet isn't shiny enough."

CHAPTER 8

I WANT THAT ONE

After Tangine had used the bathroom—complaining all the while—Amelia led him back to the dining area, where the king was slumped at the head of the table.

"That's a very grand chair, Daddy," said Tangine, pointing at the jewel-encrusted seat.

"Do you like it?" Countess Frivoleeta beamed. "It was given to me by my father. I only let very special guests use it."

King Vladimir gave what looked like a forced smile. "Very nice," he said quietly.

"It's much better than this old thing I'm sitting on," said Tangine, wriggling around. "I want a chair like that, Daddy."

"Fine, son, I'll get you one," King Vladimir said distractedly, leaning over to look at Drake's crossword puzzle.

"No, Daddy. I want *that* one," said Tangine.

"Oh, I don't think—" the countess started.

"Yes, yes, okay, it's yours," said the king, hardly seeming to listen to Tangine. "Angelkittens. That's the last clue," he said, tapping the crossword with a pointy fingernail.

Count Drake's eyes widened; then he stood up and hugged the king. "Oh, how I have MISSED you, buddy!"

Amelia couldn't contain herself any longer. "Mom! King Vladimir just told Tangine he could take YOUR chair! He didn't even ask. . . . That's stealing!"

"That's quite enough, Amelia," Countess Frivoleeta said in an unsteady voice.

"But, MOM," Amelia said.

"I said that's *quite* enough!" the countess snapped.

Wooo floated in with a platter of Curiously Crusty Crabs, Assorted Scabs and Severed Fingers on Sticks.

"Well, this looks . . . average," said Tangine, tucking a napkin into his collar. Then he took the platter from Wooo and placed it in front of himself. "But I'm too hungry to care." He shrugged and began gobbling down the food.

The whole table sat in silence while Tangine chomped and slurped, finishing with a thunderous BELCH. The king just sipped at his Sweat Shake.

"What's for dessert?" Tangine demanded, clapping his tiny hands together. A piece

of scab flew from his mouth and landed on Countess Frivoleeta's forehead.

Wooo appeared, carrying a tray of Pus-Filled Pastries. Amelia's favorite!

Again, Tangine took the whole tray. But this time Wooo was one step ahead. He disappeared through the wall and reappeared with a bigger tray of pastries, with extra pus filling! Squashy even had his own plateful. Amelia

caught Wooo's eye and smiled. He just winked and kept on serving.

At the end of the meal, the king gave a long sigh.

"Well," he said, "Tangine and I must return to the palace now."

"*The Great Gothic Gravestone Carve-Off* award ceremony is on," Tangine said.

"I-haven't-watched-the-last-episode-so-please-don't-spoil-it!" Amelia said quickly.

"Oh, so you don't know that Seth the Serpent won?" Tangine said, slyly.

Amelia was ready to throw something at him. ANYTHING . . . as long as it was heavy enough to squish him. Forever. Could this evening get any worse?

Squashy bounced onto Amelia's lap and licked her hands gently.

"That fat little orange thing shouldn't be at the table," Tangine said.

"His name is Squashy," Amelia growled.

"Daddy," said Tangine, cupping his hands under his chin. "I think I want a pet."

"You told me pets were silly," Amelia said.

"Well," Tangine said, "I changed my mind."

The king gave a sigh. "I'll get you a pet, son," he said, wrapping his cloak around his bony shoulders.

"I want a pet pumpkin," said Tangine, looking Amelia in the eyes.

Amelia felt her insides turn to ice. Squashy nuzzled closer to her chest.

"Fine," said King Vladimir. "I'll get you a pet pumpkin."

Amelia didn't take her eyes off Tangine.

Tangine grinned, showing bits of profiterole pus caught in his teeth.

"Oh no, Daddy," he said in his most superior voice. "I . . . waaaant . . . *thaaaaat* . . . oooone." And, as if in slow motion, Tangine pointed a greasy finger at Squashy.

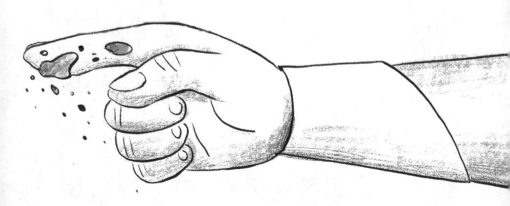

CHAPTER 9

THE GREEN DOOR WITH THE MOLDY HANDLE

Before Amelia knew it, she was running around the table to stop Tangine from getting any closer to Squashy.

"OH, DADDY! Help! I'm so scared!" Tangine wailed. He hid behind the king, then poked his head around his father's back and smirked. Amelia clenched her fists, but Countess Frivoleeta placed a hand on her shoulder.

"Amelia, calm down, please," she said quietly but firmly. "Too much pus has made you a little hysterical. . . ."

"Mom! Tell him! They can't take Squashy

away." Amelia felt tears prickling her eyes.

"Amelia, darkling," her mother said through gritted teeth. "Don't cause a scene. Remember what the king and his son have been through. It took a lot of guts for them to come out tonight. . . ."

Tangine grabbed Squashy by his stem, holding him up to his face. "You belong to *me* now."

Squashy made a tiny squeaking noise.

"Stop that!" Amelia shouted. "You're scaring him! Don't hold him like that!"

"He'll have MUCH more fun in our big palace," Tangine said.

"YOU CAN'T TAKE HIM!" Amelia reached for Squashy, who was struggling to get away from Tangine.

"Wooo, please take Amelia to her room to cool off," Countess Frivoleeta said. She looked at Amelia sadly, then cleared her throat and adjusted her hair. "We'll see our guests out."

Wooo flew over. His face usually didn't give much away, but just now he looked sad.

"You won't get away with this!" Amelia hissed into Tangine's ear as Wooo led her gently up the staircase.

"Terribly sorry about the commotion, King Vladimir," Countess Frivoleeta said. "I hope you enjoyed your evening with us. It's delightful to see you again. And, Tangine . . ." The countess forced a smile. "It's been an . . . experience."

"Wooo," Amelia whispered to the ghost butler at the top of the stairs, "I must tell Florence and Grimaldi! I have to get Squashy back!"

Wooo adjusted his eyeglass. "Now, Miss Amelia, you've been sent to your room . . . ," he said before disappearing through the wall. A moment later he reappeared with a hooded cape. "But take this, just in case you need some *fresh air*. Try to be home before the sun rises." He winked.

"Thanks, Wooo," said Amelia with a sad smile. "You're the best."

Drawing the cloak around her shoulders, she made her way to the fourth floor of the house. As she crept up the stairs, she was about to warn Squashy to keep quiet . . . but then she remembered he was gone, and her heart felt like something was squeezing it. And then she heard Tangine's slimy voice in

her mind and all she could feel was anger.

"That boy is pure unicorn poo!" she said under her breath. "I'd rather go to a thousand Barbaric Balls on my own than spend one with him!"

Amelia stared down the long corridor. Somewhere along the left-hand side was a door that led straight to the edge of the River Styx, where Grimaldi and his family lived. She had discovered it years ago when she was playing hide-and-seek with Squashy, but she could never be sure exactly which door it was.

First she tried a thin brown one with wooden carvings all over it. Stepping through, Amelia found herself in Wooo's study.

Next she tried a shiny purple door with gold trim.

"EEK!" she cried. It was one of her mother's

dressing rooms, and it was FULL of mirrors. Amelia had never seen herself from so many angles before. She backed out, feeling dizzy.

Suddenly, she felt a breeze on her ankles.

It was coming from underneath a dark green door with a moldy handle. *Hmmm,* she thought, *definitely the smell of stagnant water . . .*

She turned the creaky handle and opened the door. . . .

CHAPTER 10
STEALTHY FLORENCE

Amelia stepped into a little wooden boat that was perched on the edge of the River Styx and rowed to the Reaperton barge. She pulled up next to Grimaldi's bedroom window and knocked gently three times.

The black curtains parted, revealing Grimaldi's big eyes. They widened farther when he saw Amelia peering in, and hastily he opened the window.

"Hey . . . what's wrong?" he said, glancing at the boat. "Where's Squashy?"

"That's why I'm here," Amelia whispered. "Tangine TOOK him!"

"WHAT?" Grimaldi gasped.

"Grimmy?" came his mom's voice. "Is everything OK?"

"Er, yeah, Grimama, fine, all fine," Grimaldi yelled toward the bedroom door. "Just, er, watching a documentary about unicorns for school! It's a little scary. . . ." He glanced at Amelia hopefully. They waited in silence.

"Oh, okay," Grimaldi's mom said. "Don't stay up too late, my deathly one, and be careful not to give yourself daymares!"

"Yes, Grimamaaaa," Grimaldi said. "Sorry about that," he whispered to Amelia.

"We need to go and tell Florence before it gets too late," Amelia said. "The sun comes up soon."

Grimaldi pulled up his hood and climbed carefully into the boat.

The three friends sat under the Petrified-Tree-That-Looked-Like-a-Unicorn as Amelia explained what had happened.

"I CAN'T BELIEVE HE TOOK SQUASHY," Florence said. "WHAT A LOADA GLITTER!" She punched the ground, and an almighty crack appeared.

Amelia's heart felt heavy. "Poor Squashy," she said quietly.

Florence put a big hairy arm around Amelia's shoulders and hugged her friend to her chest. "I'LL CRUSH HIM!" she said, clenching her arm muscles in anger. "THE BIG CABBAGE BUTT!"

"You're crushing me!" Amelia wheezed through a mouthful of Florence's hair.

"OOPS, SORRY."

Amelia looked up at the sky.

"We don't have long until the sun rises, so we'll have to be fast. We need to break into the

palace," she said with a determined look on her face. "It's the only way to save Squashy!"

Grimaldi made a tiny *eep* sound.

Florence stood up and puffed her hairy chest out. "I'M IN!" she said, placing a big paw on Amelia's shoulder and almost knocking her over.

Grimaldi fiddled with the point of his hood anxiously. "What if we get caught? Or what if daylight comes before we get inside? OR WHAT IF . . ." He started hyperventilating.

"Hey," said Amelia, putting her arm around Grimaldi. "I won't let that happen.

But Squashy really needs me. Will you help me get him back?"

Grimaldi took a deep breath. "Okay . . . I'm in!"

As Amelia, Florence and Grimaldi reached Nocturnia Palace, they tried to be as quiet as possible, which was difficult for Florence.

"I CAN'T BELIEVE HOW STEALTHY I'M BEING," she said in her quietest voice, which echoed through the silence. A few crows flew out of a tree in fright.

"Shhhhh! We don't want to get caught!" Grimaldi said anxiously.

They gazed up at Nocturnia Palace, which was illuminated in the moonlight. There were hundreds of windows, all lined with black and gold.

"How are we supposed to find Squashy in there?" Grimaldi whispered.

A whiny voice floated down from a window high above them. "NO! I don't want it anymore! I'm bored with it!" Amelia would have recognized that voice anywhere. It was Tangine!

Suddenly, a heavy object came flying out the window and landed in a broken heap next to Florence.

"AARGH! I COULDA DIED!" she shouted.

"Shhh, Florence," Amelia whispered. They ducked behind a statue of the king riding a

headless chicken as Tangine's face appeared at the top window.

"Hmmm, I thought I heard something . . . ," he murmured, scanning the grounds.

Amelia took a closer look at the heap of rubble. It was the statue of Lord Ey-Ey Pistachio that Tangine had taken from her house earlier that night.

"How rude!" she muttered. "Aargh! I WISH I could fly so I could see if Squashy is in there."

"WHAT'S THE POINT IN HAVING WINGS IF YOU CAN'T USE 'EM?" said Florence.

"They're just for show, really," Amelia said with a sigh. "Like your appendix or your

tonsils. Hey, I have an idea! How about if Grimaldi balances on your shoulders, and then I climb on *his* shoulders. . . . I might be able to see in!"

"JUMP ON," Florence said, and the trio clambered over each other.

"Just a little higher . . . ," said Amelia, stretching her neck.

Florence took a deep breath and balanced on the very tips of her toes.

"Perfect!" Amelia whispered.

"I DON'T TAKE BALLET LESSONS EVERY WEEKEND FOR NOTHING," Florence said.

Through the window, Amelia could see Tangine sitting smugly on Countess Frivoleeta's chair. A tall Mummy Maid stood next to him, holding a tray of Baked Noses.

"WINIFRED! I can't hear the TV! Turn it up!"

Tangine took a Baked Nose, sniffed it, then

threw it across the room, before knocking the whole tray out of the Mummy Maid's hands. Noses scattered all over the floor, and one sneezed, launching itself into the fireplace.

"I told you I wanted SNOTTY NOSES, Winifred!" Tangine screamed. "These noses are TOO DRY! Make me some more!"

Amelia couldn't see Squashy anywhere.

"Urgh, this chair is so uncomfortable. Winifred! Wait!" Tangine stood up and kicked the chair over. "I'm sick of it now. Get rid of it." Then he clapped his hands twice. "GERALDINE!"

"Squashy's not in there. Let's try another window," Amelia whispered. Then, suddenly, she heard a familiar squeak.

CHAPTER 11

CREATURES OF THE LIGHT

Amelia had to stop herself from crying out.

A Mummy Maid had walked into the room holding Squashy, who was wearing a ruffled collar and a tiny top hat.

"Oh, you look DIVINE!" said Tangine, clapping his hands. He grabbed Squashy and plunked him on the floor. "Now, Geraldine, go and make us some Peppered Pimple Popsicles."

It took all Amelia's willpower not to climb through the window and grab Squashy. He looked so sad—he wasn't even bouncing or waggling his stem.

"Come on, Squashy. Let's do something fun!" said Tangine, bending down so his face was level with Squashy's.

Squashy turned away.

"How about a game of hide-and-seek?" Tangine beamed. He ran behind a sofa and started chuckling. "I bet you can't find me! He he he!"

Amelia watched as Squashy sighed and closed his eyes. A tiny pumpkin teardrop fell to the ground, and Amelia's heart felt like it might explode.

Tangine was still hiding behind the sofa. His smile soon turned into a frown.

"You didn't even try!" he said grumpily as he reappeared. "Okay, how about we read a book together? Do you like reading? I have a great book called *Facts About Being a Good King* . . . or another one called *Kingly Things to Do on a Rainy Day*?"

Squashy was silent.

Tangine slumped to the floor. "You're no fun," he mumbled.

Squashy suddenly started sniffing the air. Then he bounced over to the window where Amelia was perched, squeaking frantically.

No, Squashy. You're going to get me caught, Amelia thought as she quickly climbed down to the ground, leaving the sound of his pa-doings behind her.

"Did you see Squashy?" Grimaldi asked. "Is he okay?"

Florence grunted before Amelia could answer.

"AARGH. MY ARM HAIRS ARE TINGLING. SOMETHING'S WRONG!"

"Shhhh, Florence, Tangine will hear us!" Grimaldi hushed.

The sound of footsteps came from above.

"Hide!" Amelia said.

They darted behind the nearest statue just as Tangine stuck his neck out of the window. "What's all the silly fuss about, Squashy?"

Amelia could hear Squashy squeaking. It was breaking her heart to hide from him.

"Winifred!" came Tangine's voice. "Send the Gremlin Guards out to check the grounds! I think Squashy's seen something." He stared at the statue where Amelia and her friends were hiding.

"Winifred . . . ," he said.

Amelia held her breath.

"I think . . ."

Amelia's heart was pounding.

"That statue needs a clean," Tangine said as he closed the curtains.

"Phew," Amelia breathed.

"MY ARM HAIRS WON'T STOP TINGLING,"

said Florence, rubbing her biceps. "IT NEVER MEANS ANYTHING GOOD. . . ."

"Aargh!" Grimaldi squeaked, pointing toward the horizon. "The sunrise! The Creatures of the Light could appear any minute!"

"But I can't leave Squashy in there!" Amelia cried.

Grimaldi put a hand on Amelia's shoulder. "We'll get him back, I promise." Then he looked at the sky. "But if we don't hurry home we might bump into a—"

"UNICORN!"

Florence shrieked.

Emerging from the edge of the Petrified Forest, fluttering its long sparkly eyelashes

and swishing its rainbow tail, was a terrifying Creature of the Light!

"Don't let it eat me!" screamed Grimaldi,
hiding behind Florence.

The unicorn shook its rainbow mane,
sending glitter flying everywhere.

"MY EYES!" Florence shouted.

"Don't look at it directly! Avoid the sparkly
stuff!" Amelia yelled.

Grimaldi held his scythe out in front of
him, pointing it shakily at the unicorn.

"G-g-get away from us, evil c-c-creature!"
he stammered.

The unicorn trotted forward slowly.

"SQUISH IT!" Florence said.

Amelia could see that Grimaldi was trying very hard to be brave.

Then the unicorn licked the end of the scythe—and it turned into a glittery sunflower. "AAAARRRRRRRGGGH!" screamed Grimaldi, dropping it as if it were red hot.

The three friends ran as fast as they could into the Petrified Forest. Grimaldi yelped when his hood got caught on a branch.

Before Amelia could reach her friend to help him, a fluffy kitten with huge eyes and a ruffled collar swooped down. Amelia stopped dead. *If I keep really still, it might go away,* she thought.

But the tiny angel-kitten flew up to Amelia's face and started licking her nose, making strangely musical *meow* sounds.

Then, as if things couldn't get any worse, a FAIRY appeared and flew toward Grimaldi.

"AAARGGHHHH!

The worst of them all!" he screamed, just before the fairy began stroking his cheek.

"Ameeeelia!" Grimaldi shouted, but he was so scared that almost no sound came out.

Suddenly, Amelia heard a huge . . .

SPLAT!

She opened one eye. The fairy was gone.

"YEAH!" Florence said. "I AM THE MASTER OF FAIRY SQUASHING."

The angel-kitten squealed and fluttered away into the beams of sunlight.

"QUICK, IN HERE!" said Florence, leading Amelia and Grimaldi into a hole in the ground. They covered the entrance with twigs and dry leaves.

"YOU GUYS WAIT HERE. I'M GONNA DIG MY WAY THROUGH TO MY AUNT'S PIT. SHE LIVES NEARBY."

"Sorry about your scythe, Grimaldi," said Amelia, catching her breath. "You were really brave back there."

"And I'm sorry we didn't save Squashy," said Grimaldi, putting an arm around Amelia. "I promise we'll get him back."

Amelia laid her head on Grimaldi's shoulder. Florence stopped digging and shuffled her way back over.

"IT'LL ALL BE OKAY," she said, and wrapped her big hairy arms around them.

"I really hope so," Amelia said quietly, and hugged her friends tight.

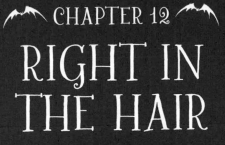

CHAPTER 12
RIGHT IN THE HAIR

"CURLY WORMS OR STRAIGHT?" Florence's aunt asked.

"BOTH!" said Florence, holding out her plate. "AUNT MAVIS MAKES THE BEST WORMS ON TOAST FOR BREAKFAST. YOU SHOULD TRY 'EM, AMELIA!"

Amelia was so tired she could barely move. She'd spent all day worrying about Squashy instead of sleeping. "I'm not very hungry, sorry."

"YOU GOT TO MAKE SURE YOU EAT," said Florence's Aunt Mavis. "OTHERWISE YOU WON'T HAVE ANY ENERGY FOR SCHOOL."

"AUNT MAVIS IS ALWAYS RIGHT," Florence said through a mouthful of worms.

"Grieving goblins!" Amelia gasped. "I need to get home before Mom discovers I've been out all day!"

"IT'S OKAY," Aunt Mavis said. "WOOO'S COVERING FOR YOU. NICE GUY."

Grimaldi looked worried.

"AND DON'T WORRY, GRIMALDI. I TOLD YOUR GRIMPAPA YOU WERE DEALING WITH A TOAD-SQUASHING DISASTER. FIFTEEN DEAD. FIVE WITHOUT LEGS."

Grimaldi relaxed. "Ah, thank you, Mavis."

Amelia managed to eat a few spoonfuls of worms. She was about to grab a handful for Squashy to munch on later but stopped and felt her heart sink again. Grimaldi scooped up some worms and slipped them into Amelia's backpack.

"Squashy's going to be hungry when we

get him back. . . ." He smiled, and the three friends set off for school.

Amelia waited at the entrance of the academy for Tangine. He was late again. Florence and Grimaldi insisted on staying with her.

"It's okay, guys, I don't want you getting in trouble too," Amelia said.

"NAH, IT'S FINE," Florence said. "WE'RE STICKING BY YOU."

"That's what friends are for, right?" Grimaldi smiled—but Amelia could tell he was a bit worried about getting yelled at.

Amelia turned to see the scraggly vulture with three eyes landing with a clunk.

SQUAAAAAWK!

Tangine jumped down from its back and sauntered over to Amelia and her friends.

"What are wannabe-Death and the beast doing here?" he said, folding his arms.

Florence growled.

"Don't call Florence that," Amelia said. "And where's Squashy?"

"Back at the palace, silly," Tangine said. "You shouldn't bring pets to school! I don't know how you ever got away with it."

"You're being really mean," Grimaldi said in a small voice. Confrontation was one of his biggest fears.

"Garibaldi, isn't it?" Tangine said, raising an eyebrow.

"No, it's Grim—" Grimaldi began.

"It must be hard juggling school and death *and* sneaking around, eh?" Tangine interrupted. Then he clapped twice. "SHAUN! Bring the *thing*. . . ."

A Mummy Maid came running over and held up a wilting glittery sunflower that had half morphed back into a scythe.

Tangine didn't even seem to notice all the disgusting glitter. He just dropped the sunflower scythe to the ground in front of Grimaldi. Then he turned to Amelia. "You look awfully tired. Were you up all day?"

Amelia felt a wave of panic.

"And finally, if it isn't the beast," Tangine sneered at Florence.

"I TOLD YOU I AM NOT A BEAST. I'M A RARE BREED OF—" Florence started.

But before she could finish, Tangine held a handful of long white hairs under her nose.

"These were found on the palace grounds when I woke up this evening. They are the hairs of a rare breed of yeti." He raised both eyebrows. "So it would be very

unfortunate if you were this particular breed of yeti, *hmmm?*" Tangine frowned. "Trespassing on palace grounds is a punishable offense. So what's it going to be?"

For the first time in her life, Florence spoke at a normal volume. "Beast. I'm a . . . beast."

"Oh, then these hairs can't possibly belong to you . . . beast," said Tangine, sprinkling Florence's hairs over Grimaldi's head.

"AMELIA FANG!" Miss Inspine burst out of the Catacomb Academy entrance. "Where is the prince? Oh, bothersome boogies, if we've lost—"

She caught sight of Tangine and heaved such a big sigh of relief that her skull fell off.

"Florence, Grimaldi, why aren't you in class?" Her headless skeleton put a hand on its hip. "This is unacceptable! And, Amelia Fang, you've made the prince late for class YET again! I'm starting to think Frankie would make a better host, you know. . . ."

"Sorry, Miss Inspine. It won't happen again," Amelia said through gritted teeth.

"Yeah, Ameeelia," said Tangine, folding his arms. "You're supposed to be setting a

good example. I guess you *would* pick up bad habits hanging out with a beast."

And then Florence reached out and rubbed the top of his head hard. The hairs that had been slicked back were now sticking out in every direction. "WHO LOOKS LIKE A BEAST NOW?"

Miss Inspine was so shocked that her whole skeleton disconnected into a big pile of bones.

The Mummy Maid named Shaun picked Tangine up and carried him inside.

"Aaaaargh! Is he okay?" Miss Inspine spluttered from the ground. Then she glared at Amelia, Florence and Grimaldi. "That's SIX months detention for all three of you! And get to class, NOW!"

Once Miss Inspine had managed to reconnect her bones and Tangine had spent an hour being pampered by the Mummy

Maids to get his hair back into shape, the class settled down ready for their Repugnant Recipes lesson.

"Tonight, class," Miss Inspine said, "you will be making Fingernail-Clipping Cakes and Toe Jam. Remember to dig deep under those toenails and get out all the goodness!"

Amelia, Florence, Grimaldi and Tangine sat in silence. The air was thick with tension and the smell of feet.

"Squashy and I are having such fun, you know," said Tangine, twiddling his thumbs. "We even played hide-and-seek together."

Amelia was too angry to speak.

Tangine frowned. "Squashy LOVES the palace. There's sooo much room to bounce around!"

Amelia stared down at the bowl of toenail clippings. Her heart ached.

"How can you miss that useless pumpkin so much?" Tangine snapped.

Amelia's eyes were watery and her voice was wobbly. "Because I love him more than anything," she said quietly. "You wouldn't understand, though, because you only seem to care about yourself."

Tangine looked shocked, and he started twiddling his thumbs even more furiously. Then he sat up straight and folded his arms.

"Oh, come on! Just ask your mom and dad to buy you a new one. That's what I would do."

Amelia's voice was shaking. "That is because you don't know the TRUE value of things," she said. "You're a SPOILED SPROUT!"

CHAPTER 13
INTESTINE!

Amelia arrived home feeling tired and fed up after an hour of scrubbing goblin slime off the classroom walls. She closed her bedroom door behind her and leaned against the cold wood. Then she gave a huge sigh and slid down to the floor.

"Miss Amelia," came Wooo's voice from behind the door.

"Come in, Wooo," Amelia said wearily, moving aside.

Wooo appeared, holding a tray of Amelia's favorite Tongue-Twister Sandwiches.

"Aw, thanks, Wooo," she said, taking a sandwich. She hadn't realized how hungry she was. "Oh, Wooo." She chewed a

mouthful. "I don't know what to do! I just want Squashy back."

"Hmmm," said Wooo, adjusting his eyeglass. "Can't you visit your 'new friend' at the palace? Then *how you spend* your visit is up to you. . . ."

Amelia stopped chewing. "Wooo, you are a genius!"

"You know where I am if you need me." Wooo winked, disappearing through the wall.

Amelia rushed out of her bedroom and raced along the long corridor. "Mooooom!" she called. "Where are you? I need to ask you something!"

"Yes, darkling?" came her mother's voice. "I'm in my dressing room!"

"Which one?" asked Amelia, looking at the rows of doors.

"Last door on the left!" her mom called.

Amelia ran to the end of the corridor and opened a shiny black door. She stepped inside. "Mom— Oh."

Count Drake was hanging upside down from a shelf, engrossed in a crossword puzzle.

"INTESTINE!" he yelled, and fell off the shelf into a pile of crossword books.

Amelia shook her head and stepped back into the corridor, closing the door behind her.

"MOM! The doors have moved again. Where are you?" she called.

"Try the next floor up . . . ," her mom's voice echoed.

Amelia was growing impatient. "I just wanted to ask if I could visit Tangine at the palace," she called. "Y'know, to hang out . . . like friends do?"

Suddenly, a door at the other end of the corridor burst open and Countess Frivoleeta emerged, wearing the frilliest dress Amelia had ever seen. Amelia tried not to giggle. Her mom pranced down the corridor, making the frills flap like spare body parts.

"Amelia, my little darkling of hope, what a delightful idea!" Countess Frivoleeta said.

"So I can go?" Amelia said.

"Of course! Spend as much time at the palace as you like. Oh, I'm so glad you and the prince are friends now. You never know! Maybe one day you'll get—"

"Okay, Mom, BYE!" Amelia slipped away quickly before her mom could finish. She slid down the banister of the spiral staircase, feeling more hopeful. She was finally going to get Squashy back!

CHAPTER 12

KING VLADIMIR'S SECRET

When Amelia arrived at the palace, a Gremlin Guard came rushing over.

"What's your business here?" he grunted.

"Um, I'm here to see Tangine. We go to school together. The king knows my dad, Count Drake, really well. I'm Amelia Fang." She held her breath while the Gremlin Guard scrunched up his face, looking at Amelia suspiciously. The silence seemed to last forever.

"Very well," he barked at last. "This way."

The guard led Amelia across the courtyard toward a huge golden door. It took fifteen

Mummy Maids to pull it open. Just as Amelia slipped inside, a loud scream rang out.

"AAAAAAAAAAAAARRRGGGHHH!!!!"

Amelia jumped in fright.

"The Scream Tea is ready!" the Mummy Maids shouted. "We will prepare you a cup. Why are you here, young vampire?"

"I've come to see Tangine," Amelia said.

"He's just having his nightly elbow exfoliation. You can wait in here." A Mummy Maid led Amelia into the drawing room and then shuffled out, closing the door behind her.

Amelia gazed at her surroundings. In the middle of the vast room was an enormous black sofa with a row of sharp teeth. The walls were lined with golden bookcases and fancy cabinets.

In the corner stood a statue of Tangine, which was much taller than the real thing.

Amelia reached up and poked it on the nose. Something creaked—and a wall moved slowly to the left, revealing a narrow doorway.

Amelia gasped. *A quick look won't hurt,* she thought. She checked to make sure the coast was clear and stepped through.

Inside, the walls were covered with framed portraits and shelf upon shelf of ancient-looking books. Amelia walked over to a wooden desk covered in a thick layer of dust.

There was a leather-bound book on the

desk, with the corner of something sticking out from the crinkled pages. Amelia slid it out, then gasped again. It was a photograph. Taking a deep breath, she stared down at the image in her shaking hand.

The man in the picture was King Vladimir. But a much younger and happier King Vladimir. He was holding a tiny baby, who Amelia guessed must be Tangine. Next to the king hovered a small, shimmering lady with white flowing hair and GLITTER all over her big patterned . . . FAIRY WINGS.

There was no denying it. She was a terrifying Creature of the Light!

"Peculiar pumpkins!" Amelia shuddered. "This can only mean one thing. . . ."

Amelia looked closer at baby Tangine. His hair was white and sparkling, and on his back was a pair of tiny fairy wings. "Tangine is half Creature of the Light!" she breathed.

Amelia picked up the book that had held the photograph. She wiped the front cover with her sleeve. The words

Vlad's Book of Special Memories

appeared in swirling golden letters. Amelia's heart was pounding. She opened the diary carefully. Inside, she found more photos of King Vladimir and the fairy.

Then, a few pages in, Amelia came across some diary entries.

I am completely and utterly head over heels in love. Today, I'm going to ask Fairyweather if she will marry me.

Amelia's eyes widened.

I've made us a picnic to enjoy in the Petrified Forest at dusk. She said she'd try

some Grilled Guts as long as I'd try some Sweet Sparkle Swirls. To be honest, I'd love anything Fairyweather made me. She's the most kind-hearted creature I've ever known.

Amelia turned the page, to find more pictures of King Vladimir and the fairy—who, Amelia realized, must be Fairyweather. The more Amelia looked at the fairy, the less scary she seemed. She had a kind, happy face—nothing like the awful fairies in the books Amelia had read at school.

Today Fairyweather and I got married by the Wishing Well of Well-Wishes in the Meadow of Loveliness. The Wishing Well was rather rude, and splashed water at me, but I was far too happy to care!

I want to announce our love to everyone, but Fairyweather is worried she won't be accepted. The Nocturnians still believe that Creatures of the Light are terrifying and dangerous. I can't blame them. We've been taught to fear the Creatures of the Light for generations. But now I know the truth. I just wish I could prove it to the rest of Nocturnia. I can't even tell my best friend, Drake.

Amelia sat still, unable to turn the page.

All her life she had believed that Creatures of the Light were frightful beings that wanted to cause Nocturnians harm. She had been just as scared of them as everyone else.

We are so happy! We've had the pudgiest, ugliest baby and I am overwhelmed with love! He looks a little like a squashed pumpkin right now, but I'm sure he'll take after his beautiful mother and grow into a dashing young man! We've decided to call him Tangine Fairyweather La Floofle the First. But to the rest of Nocturnia, he shall be known as Prince Tangine the First. The kingdom can't know about his mother just yet.

The next ten pages were full of photos of Tangine as a baby, then a toddler.

Amelia thought he actually looked cute without that smug grin plastered on his face. He was hugging his parents in almost every photograph. Amelia wondered how such a sweet little boy could have turned into such a mean, spoiled sprout.

She read on . . .

I can barely write. Fairyweather has gone. She didn't even leave a note.

Everything was perfect. We went for a lovely morning walk yesterday. She was so excited to finally show Nocturnia the truth about the Creatures of the Light. But later that night, I couldn't find her anywhere. . . .

I just don't understand. What will I tell poor little Tangine? I have to find her. . . .

The words looked like drops of water had smudged them. The pictures on the next pages showed Tangine looking sad and lonely. The king wasn't in any of them. Instead, Tangine was surrounded by Mummy Maids, and in every photo he had more and more toys. As the years went on, his face became dark and troubled. His fairy wings

were covered with a cape, and his hair was dyed, to hide the sparkles.

We've been invited to the Fangs' Barbaric Ball again this year, but I can't bring myself to go. I need to find Fairyweather! The pain is still as fresh as last night's cabbage froth.

I've been searching for her every hour of every night while the Kingdom of the Light sleeps. If I risk going during the day, I'll be spotted. It appears that the Creatures of the Light are just as scared of us as we are of them.

But I won't give up until I find Fairyweather. The Mummy Maids are taking care of Tangine in my absence. I fear for him, though. I don't want him to be judged for his Creature-of-the-Light blood.

Maybe I've got Tangine all wrong, thought Amelia. *It must have been hard growing up without a mom, and his dad doesn't seem to spend any time with him.* Amelia knew how lonely that could be. *Her* dad would sometimes rather do crosswords than play with her. But at least she had Squashy and her friends. *Who did Tangine have?*

CHAPTER 15
FRIEND

"Amelia Fang is here?" Tangine's voice came from the drawing room. He sounded surprised—and pleased.

Amelia quickly closed the diary and peered around the secret doorway.

Tangine was sitting on the sofa, swinging his legs.

"PAULA!" he yelled.

A Mummy Maid came running in.

"You're *sure* Amelia Fang is here to see me?" he asked.

"That's what she said," the Mummy Maid replied.

"*Hmmm.* Maybe she wants to be friends after all." He smiled. It wasn't a sneer

or a smirk. It was a real smile. Amelia felt
a little sorry for him again. He looked very
small and lonely sitting in the middle of
the huge room.

But she couldn't forget why she was here.
She had to get Squashy back.

"So where IS she?" Tangine called. He slid off the chair and wandered out of the room.

Amelia ran back in, and jumped onto the sofa.

"OUCH!" she yelped as the sofa bit her butt.

Tangine's head popped around the door. "Oh, there you are," he said, looking confused.

"Er, hi!" Amelia said.

She was still trying to piece everything together, but it was all slowly becoming clear: the reason Tangine was so short while the king was so tall, the glitter he'd had on his shoe when he visited Amelia's house and the fact that he hadn't minded holding Grimaldi's glittery sunflower scythe.

"I didn't expect you to visit me," said Tangine, interrupting her thoughts.

"Well, since we're at school together, I thought it would be . . . fun," said Amelia, faking a smile.

Tangine's eyes lit up.

"Umm, where's Squashy?" Amelia asked.

Tangine frowned. "He's having his dinner

right now." Then his expression changed. "How about we play a board game? I have a new one called Full Moonopoly. Or we could play Bat Trap! That's a good one. No fun to play by yourself, but now that you're here . . ." He started rummaging around in a cabinet.

"Maybe we could wait for Squashy?" Amelia asked hopefully. "He could join in."

Tangine emerged from the cabinet and started twiddling his thumbs. "I thought you came here to hang out with ME, Amelia." He was frowning again.

"Where is Squashy, Tangine?" said Amelia, beginning to lose her patience. "I really want to see him!"

"Squashy, Squashy, Squashy," Tangine said in a high-pitched voice. His face was going red. "It's all about Squashy! You didn't

come here to see me at all, did you? You just came here to take Squashy back!" He folded his arms. "I thought you wanted to be my friend."

Amelia looked at the floor. Any sympathy she'd felt toward Tangine after reading the diary was draining away.

"You should go," Tangine said. "Mindy will see you out."

Amelia sighed. Deep down in that dark, spoiled boy there HAD to be some kindness. SOMEWHERE. She thought about the photographs of the happy toddler. But she couldn't let herself feel sorry for Tangine. She needed to speak to Florence and Grimaldi. They would help her come up with a new plan to rescue Squashy.

Back at the Fang Mansion, Amelia tiptoed up the staircase to the fourth floor and found the green door with its moldy handle. She opened the door, jumped straight into the little boat on the River Styx and rowed to the Reapertons' barge. Grimaldi was sitting outside with a shiny new scythe, chatting to half a worm.

"Hey, Amelia!" Grimaldi waved. "Look! Dad got me a new scythe!"

"Cool," Amelia said quickly. "But jump in! We need to get Florence and make a new plan. Tangine won't give Squashy back!"

"Oh, that big unicorn-face!" said Grimaldi, clenching his fists.

Amelia and Grimaldi arrived at the Spudwick Pit, where Florence was busy doing one-armed push-ups.

"HELLO, GUYS!" she puffed. "WANNA SIT ON MY BACK WHILE I EXERCISE? I'M

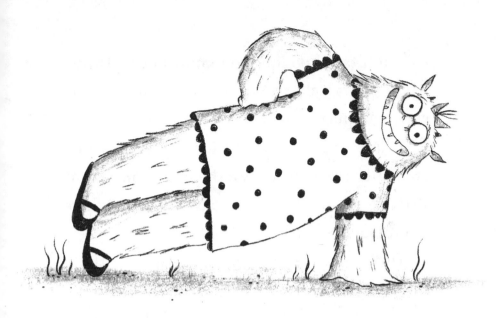

BUILDING UP MY MUSCLES FOR WHEN I HELP DAD WITH PIT-DIGGING FOR HALLOWEEN." She flexed her arms, revealing an impressive set of biceps.

"Sorry to disturb your training, Florence," Amelia said, "but it's an emergency!"

Amelia was about to tell her friends about Tangine's secret. But then she stopped herself. She wasn't sure how she felt about the Creatures of the Light now, and

it would take too long to explain everything. Right now she had to concentrate on getting Squashy back.

"Okay," she said. "Both King Vladimir and Tangine are coming to the ball tomorrow. THAT'S our chance to go to Nocturnia Palace and rescue Squashy."

"How will we get to the palace without anyone seeing us?" Grimaldi said.

"I COULD DIG US A TUNNEL FROM THE RIVER SO NOBODY SPOTS US ABOVEGROUND," Florence said.

"Florence, that is the BEST idea ever!" said Amelia, trying to high-five her friend but missing because she couldn't quite reach.

"What if Tangine spots you sneaking off?" Grimaldi asked.

"Good point. I'll need something to keep him busy," Amelia said thoughtfully.

"WHY DON'T YOU LEAD HIM INTO ONE

OF YOUR DOORS AND MAKE SURE HE GETS STUCK IN THERE?" Florence suggested.

"Stuck . . . ," Amelia muttered. "Now, that gives me an idea!"

"OOOH, I LOVE A GOOD PLAN!" Florence said. "MAKES ME FEEL LIKE A SECRET AGENT OR SOMETHING."

"Okay, guys, I'll see you both at the River Styx tomorrow at midnight!" said Amelia. "And leave Tangine to me."

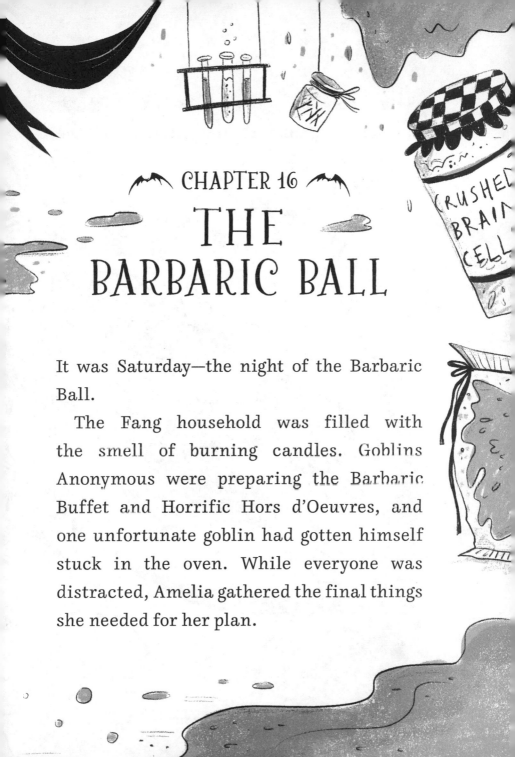

CHAPTER 16
THE
BARBARIC BALL

It was Saturday—the night of the Barbaric Ball.

The Fang household was filled with the smell of burning candles. Goblins Anonymous were preparing the Barbaric Buffet and Horrific Hors d'Oeuvres, and one unfortunate goblin had gotten himself stuck in the oven. While everyone was distracted, Amelia gathered the final things she needed for her plan.

The doorbell gong bellowed through the house, marking the arrival of the first guests.

"IT BEGIIIINS!" Countess Frivoleeta squealed.

Wooo whizzed past her and greeted a group of serpents in huge ruffled collars who were waiting at the front door. In their excitement, they had managed to tie themselves in knots. Wooo led them to the ballroom at the back of the house.

Back in her bedroom, Amelia felt her heart jump with joy at the thought of rescuing Squashy.

Suddenly, Countess Frivoleeta came bursting in.

"Amelia!" she bellowed. "Stop hanging around in the shadows and get to the ballroom this instant. Haven't you learned anything from your vampiress etiquette lessons?"

"Yes, Mom." Amelia walked as elegantly as she could out of the bedroom.

Countess Frivoleeta cooed in excitement. "Oh, my dreariest, you look revoltingly RAVISHING! I am so proud!"

As Amelia walked to the ballroom, she heard the thumping beats and *AAAAH OOOOOOOO*s of the Howling Wolf Band. She edged to the back of the room, trying not to draw attention to herself.

SQUAAAAAWK!
CRASH!

"YOU STUPID BIRD! YOU'RE FIRED!" Tangine's voice echoed through the house. The Howling Wolf Band stopped howling,

and the crowd gathered around the black carpet, murmuring excitedly.

The huge ballroom doors swung open and Wooo made the announcement:

"Count and Countess Fang are delighted to welcome some VERY special guests to the Barbaric Ball. After many years of absence, I present: KING VLADIMIR the THIRTEENTH!"

The crowd erupted. One skeleton fell apart with excitement.

King Vladimir walked in. His face was solemn, and his eyes had dark rings around them. He headed straight for the buffet, waving half-heartedly at the crowd as he passed.

"And now for our NEXT special guest!" announced Wooo. "Our future king . . . TANGERINE!"

Tangine stopped midmarch and furrowed his brows. "It's TanGEEEEN!" he hissed.

"Oh, I'm terribly sorry, Tanning Cream," said Wooo.

"No! TANGINE, you transparent turnip!"

"I do beg your pardon," said Wooo. "Follow me, Tin Bean."

"AAARRRRGH!" Tangine gritted his teeth and marched along behind Wooo.

"Let's hear it for TAMBORIIIINE!" said Wooo, and the crowd exploded with cheers and claps and slime.

Tangine shook his head and walked straight through Wooo in anger. Walking through a ghost was the highest level of insult.

The Howling Wolf Band started playing the "Dance Macabre."

Amelia checked the clock. It was almost midnight. Maybe she could sneak out without Tangine seeing her. . . .

"Oh, Ameeelia," came his familiar voice.

Amelia's heart fell to the tips of her pointy black boots. "Oh, hey, Tangine," she said, trying to sound cheerful.

"I'm still angry with you," he said, folding his arms. "And Squashy isn't here, before you ask."

Amelia kept calm. "Look, I'm sorry if I offended you last night . . . but I really hate dancing, and I've always wanted someone

to hang out with at this boring ball! How
about we play a game?"

Tangine frowned. "Is this another trick?"

"What about tag?" said Amelia, ignoring
his question.

Tangine narrowed his eyes.

"TAG! You're it!" Amelia tapped his arm,
then ran off before he could stop her.

"What? Hey! Come back!" Tangine said,
then ran after her. When she looked back over
her shoulder, Amelia saw his frown slowly

turning into a smile.

Amelia led Tangine down the staircase, away from the party. They passed a sprite tugging at a plate that was stuck to his face with goblin slime.

"Wait for me!" Tangine puffed. Giggling, he followed Amelia down a corridor, through a huge door and into complete darkness.

"Amelia?" he called, his laughter fading. "Where are you? I thought we were playing tag . . . not hide-and-seek!"

Amelia hesitated, catching her breath in the dark. "I'm sorry, Tangine," she said, before throwing a bucketful of goblin slime over his head.

SPLOSH!

"AAAAAAARGGGHHH!"

Tangine yelled. "WHAT'S GOING ON? I can't see a thing!"

SPLOSH!

"GAAAAAAAAAH! I can't move!"

he bellowed as the goblin slime set like concrete. "Get me out of here this instant!"

The more he struggled, the more the slime hardened around him. "This isn't how you play tag, Amelia! What's going on?"

"I'm really sorry, but you've given me no choice . . . ," Amelia whispered. Then she stepped out and shut the door behind her.

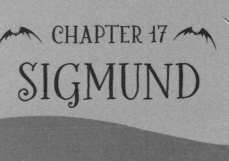

CHAPTER 17
SIGMUND

Amelia made her way to the green door with the moldy handle and found Florence and Grimaldi waiting on the other side. She felt terrible for trapping Tangine, but it was her only chance to get Squashy back.

"Let's go," Amelia said. "Florence, are you ready to dig like you've never dug before?"

"ALREADY DONE IT." Florence grinned. "YOUR UNDERGROUND PASSAGE TO THE PALACE AWAITS."

"Excellent job!" Amelia said.

"It was amazing," Grimaldi said. "Florence is a MACHINE!"

As the friends entered the tunnel, Grimaldi tapped his scythe and PING! It began to glow a luminous green.

"Whoa!" Amelia said. "That's one fancy new scythe."

"I know, right?" Grimaldi said. "It glows three different colors!"

The friends pressed on, and the tunnel got darker. . . .

"How much farther, Florence?" Amelia asked.

Florence sniffed the air. "'BOUT THREE YARDS . . ."

She paused and tapped at the mud above her head. Amelia gasped as it fell away to reveal an opening.

Florence poked her head through the hole, then crouched back down. "LOOKS LIKE THE PALACE KITCHEN— FULL OF MUMMY MAIDS!"

"Okay," Amelia said. "Let's do this. You happy to keep watch, Florence?"

"ON IT." Her friend smiled.

"And, Grimaldi, are you ready?" Amelia said.

"I've been face to face with a unicorn," he replied. "I don't think anything could scare me more than that!" He beamed. "Except maybe ladybirds."

Amelia and Grimaldi coughed and spluttered as they emerged in the kitchen fireplace, covered in soot. Mummy Maids were scurrying about with overflowing plates and bowls. None of them noticed that a vampire and a grim reaper had just crawled into the kitchen.

Amelia and Grimaldi hid behind a shelf of jars full of various body parts.

"How are we supposed to get through without being seen?" Amelia whispered.

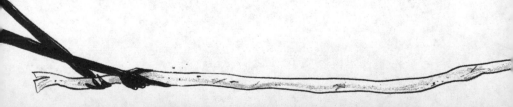

"There are Mummy Maids EVERYWHERE."

"Hey, I have an idea!" said Grimaldi, grabbing the end of a piece of grubby white cloth. The cloth was attached to a Mummy Maid, who began slowly unraveling as he moved around the kitchen.

The other maids started screaming and throwing dishes at the naked Mummy Maid. "OUTRAGEOUS!" yelled one, gripping a test tube so tightly it smashed. A nude Mummy Maid is not a pretty sight—all

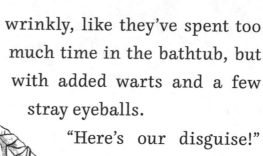

wrinkly, like they've spent too much time in the bathtub, but with added warts and a few stray eyeballs.

"Here's our disguise!" Grimaldi grinned. "Climb on my shoulders and hold the end of the cloth."

Amelia sat on Grimaldi's shoulders while he twirled around, wrapping them both in the cloth until they looked like one very tall Mummy Maid.

Grimaldi wobbled his way through the kitchen, knocking over a few pots

in the process. Amelia tapped his head and whispered, "Should we ask one of the Mummy Maids if they know where Squashy is?"

"Good idea!" Grimaldi said. "Let's try this one." He headed over to a very fat Mummy Maid who was mixing up a bowl of sludge.

"Oh, Sigmund!" the Mummy Maid rasped. "So glad you're here! Could you be a dear and fetch that packet of Splattered Spleen from the top shelf?"

"Er, sure," said Amelia, putting on a deep voice. She grabbed the most splattery-looking thing from the shelf.

"Thank you, Sigmund! Actually, while you're here, perhaps you could fetch me some boogie bundles from Debra? I think this dish could do with a touch of boogie."

Amelia was getting impatient. "Uh, so

that pumpkin, Squashy . . . where's he at these days?" she blurted out.

The Mummy Maid tutted. "I'd completely forgotten about that silly pumpkin! I was supposed to feed him ages ago!"

Amelia flinched, and a piece of cloth came loose at her nose.

"Would you feed him for me?" said the Mummy Maid, not looking up. "He's in the cellar."

Amelia couldn't believe her luck! She tried to stay calm and balanced on Grimaldi's shoulders.

Suddenly, the real Sigmund shouted from across the kitchen, "HEY! That's not a Mummy Maid!"

Grimaldi didn't wait to hear what was coming next. He ran as fast as he could, the cloth fast unraveling from around them. Amelia spotted a wooden trapdoor and

yanked it open. A rickety staircase stretched down into complete darkness.

"Smells like a cellar to me!" said Grimaldi.

They jumped through the trapdoor. . . .

CHAPTER 18

I AM NOT A BEAST!

Amelia couldn't see a thing.

"Hold on . . . ," said Grimaldi, and the next second the cellar was lit up by the scythe's green glow.

The cellar was a treasure trove of grotesque ingredients—from pots of earwax, bags of knees and inside-out brains to feet with eyeballs as toes.

When Squashy spotted Amelia, he squeaked louder than he'd ever squeaked before and bounced straight into her arms with one big pa-doing!

Amelia hugged him tightly. "Oh, Squashy! I'm SO happy to see you!" Squashy licked the tears that were running down Amelia's cheeks.

"Um . . . Amelia . . ." Grimaldi nudged her.

The trapdoor crashed inward, and a group of angry Mummy Maids appeared.

"There they are! Get them!" Sigmund shouted. "And that pumpkin!"

Squashy started squeaking in fear, but Amelia couldn't see a way out of the cellar.

Sigmund reached for Grimaldi's scythe.

"Get off!" Grimaldi shouted. "This is BRAND-NEW!" The scythe was flashing from green to orange to purple, so the cellar looked like some kind of disco.

Amelia picked up a stray eyeball-toed

foot and launched it through the air. It hit Sigmund in the forehead.

But other Mummy Maids were flooding in thick and fast.

How could they escape?

CRASH!

Pots of earwax went splattering into the Mummy Maids' faces. Noses and eyeball-toed feet went flying as the ground exploded, and from the dust and dirt emerged a big, hairy figure.

"BEEEEEAST!" the Mummy Maids cried.

"I AM NOT A BEAST!" Florence yelled. "I'M A RARE . . ." She punched one Mummy Maid in the foot. "BREED . . ." Then she punched another Mummy Maid in the armpit. "OF YETI!"

"FLORENCE!" Amelia and Grimaldi cried together.

"MY ARM HAIRS WERE TINGLING. FIGURED I BEST INVESTIGATE," said Florence, holding a Mummy Maid up by her toes. The other Mummy Maids were closing in, looking very angry.

"I GOT THIS!" Florence shouted.

"YOU GUYS GET
OUT OF HERE!"
Amelia held
Squashy tight and grabbed
Grimaldi's hand, and they raced
into the tunnel as fast as they
could. Florence rolled up her sleeves
and flexed her muscles.
"Move it, BEAST!"
Sigmund shouted.

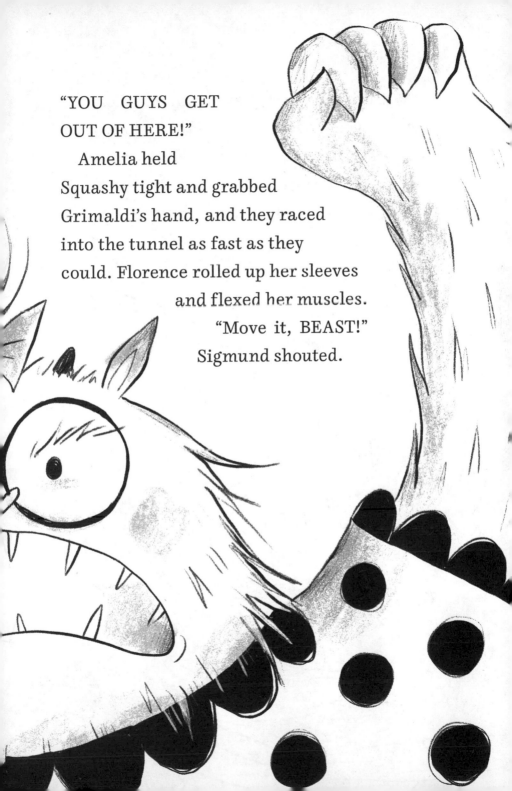

With one more giant punch, Florence sent every Mummy Maid sprawling. Then, with the grace of a hippopotamus ballerina, she pirouetted around the stunned maids and tied them together using their own cloth.

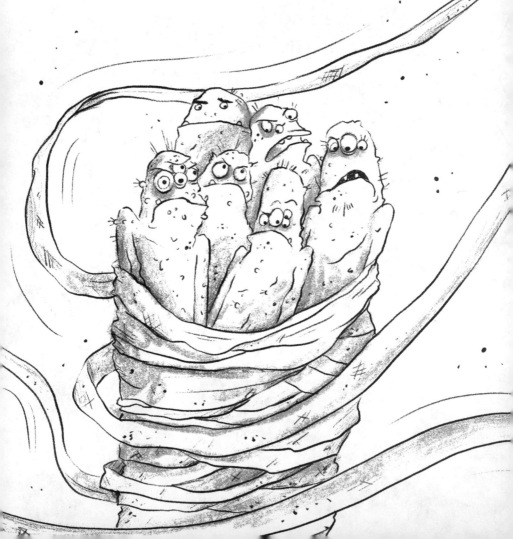

CHAPTER 19
DOOR CHASE

Amelia, Grimaldi and Squashy finally emerged aboveground at the edge of the River Styx. Amelia held Squashy close, and even in the cold night air, she felt nothing but warmth. Squashy nuzzled closer, making little squeaks.

Florence caught up with them. She hadn't even broken a sweat. "OY, GRIMALDI, YOU CAN TURN YOUR SCYTHE LIGHT OFF NOW," she said.

"It won't turn off," said Grimaldi, fiddling with the settings. "I think those Mummy Maids broke it."

Amelia could hear the music coming from the Fang Mansion in the distance.

"I should get back to the ball before anyone misses me!" she said. "Thank you both for helping me get Squashy back."

Florence threw her arms around Amelia and Grimaldi, and the scythe lit up her fur.

"WAIT. . . ." Florence gulped. "IS THAT . . . GLITTER?"

Squashy squeaked in fear and hid behind Amelia's legs.

A patch of glitter sparkled on the ground as the silhouette of a small boy came into view.

"Tangine!" Amelia said. Her brain was racing. How on earth had he escaped from all that goblin slime?

"I thought we were playing tag," Tangine said quietly.

"WHAT'S HE SAYING?" Florence bellowed. "WHY'S HE BEING SO QUIET?"

"I'm sorry, Tangine," Amelia said softly.

"But you left me with no other option. Why wouldn't you give Squashy back?"

Tangine twiddled his thumbs. "I just . . . didn't want to." He shrugged. "I needed a pet to play with, since nobody wanted to be my friend. And you were always going on about how great Squashy is." His shoulders drooped. "Turns out Squashy didn't want to play with me either."

"Tangine, you've been treating us more like your servants than your friends," Amelia said. "And you're horrible to *them*. Friends don't order each other around, and they don't steal each other's things."

"But that's what I do with the Mummy Maids." Tangine looked confused.

"Well, you shouldn't. And you're supposed to share with your friends," Amelia went on. "Friends are kind to each other. Nobody wants to be friends with someone

who's mean to them!" She sighed. "Look, I saw something in your dad's study when I came to visit last night. . . ."

Tangine frowned. "Daddy hasn't used his study in years. Why were you in there?"

"WHY IS THERE GLITTER ALL AROUND HIM?" said Florence, striding forward.

"It's okay, Florence," said Amelia, blocking her way. Squashy started squeaking.

Florence and Grimaldi exchanged a confused look.

Amelia stepped forward. "Tangine . . . I know. I know your secret."

A look of panic flashed across Tangine's face.

Amelia turned to her friends. "I didn't want to tell you guys, because I wanted to concentrate on getting Squashy back. And I wasn't sure you'd understand." Then she turned to face Tangine. "I know who your mother is."

"Um, Amelia . . . his mother was eaten," Grimaldi whispered. "By a *fairy*!"

Tangine didn't move.

"That's not true," Amelia said. "Tangine's mother disappeared, but she wasn't eaten by a fairy. . . . She IS a fairy!"

"WHAT?" Florence bellowed.

Grimaldi yelped.

Tangine stood quietly in the floating doorway. Amelia couldn't help noticing how small and helpless he looked.

"No, no," Amelia started. "The Creatures of the Light aren't evi—"

"AARGHH! HE'S A CREATURE OF THE LIGHT!" Florence yelled, charging toward Tangine.

"No! STOP, FLORENCE!" Amelia shouted. But before she knew it, Florence and Tangine were both tumbling through the floating doorway, back into the Fang Mansion.

"FLORENCE!" Amelia cried, leaping through the door after them. "Stop, Florence! You don't understand!"

But it was no use.

Tangine ran through a door at the end of the corridor, then reappeared through a small yellow one, in front of Amelia and Grimaldi.

"Tangine!" Amelia said. "It's okay." But Tangine looked terrified and ran back through the door.

Florence came pounding down the corridor.

"DON'T WORRY, GUYS. I'LL SAVE YOU FROM THAT MONSTROUS CREATURE!" She squeezed herself through the small yellow door before Amelia could stop her.

Amelia and Grimaldi dived after her and found themselves in a room full of yet more doors. Tangine leapt through a pink door and slammed it behind him. The door popped into a thousand pink bubbles.

"OH, MAN!" Florence thundered, punching the bubbles. "YOUR DOORS ARE NOT HELPING!"

"Florence!" Amelia said. "Listen to me!"

"I LOST THE LITTLE SCRUMP!" said Florence, dusting herself down.

"THERE!" Grimaldi yelled.

Tangine emerged from a hexagonal door on the other side of the room. When he spotted Florence, he tried to turn back, but the door had locked itself. Tangine tried the next door down.

Florence bounded over, grunting with every step.

"GUYS! You have to stop!" Amelia cried. Squashy was bouncing up and down in panic.

Tangine backed away from Florence and bumped into a huge stripy door. He tried turning the handle, but it wouldn't open.

"GAH!" he yelled in frustration. "Stupid doors!" He kicked the next door.

It kicked him back.

Florence pounced. Tangine looked from side to side in terror, then blew a mouthful of glitter in Florence's face.

"AAAAAARGH! MY EYES!" Florence cried.

A huge cloud of glitter spread across the room. Grimaldi dropped his scythe and waved his hands around in horror. "The SPARKLY stuff! It's in my mouth!" he squealed, and then gagged.

Florence made a lunge for Tangine, but Amelia threw herself in front of him. Squashy followed, trying to protect Amelia, and Grimaldi tried to grab Squashy. Before they knew it, the five of them were tumbling through a big swirly door and falling down,

      down,

        down,

          until . . .

THUD!

Amelia groaned and looked up to see her mother's startled face.

They had landed smack-dab in the middle of the Barbaric Ball.

Squashy went rolling across the length of the ballroom with one big SQUEEEEEEEEEEEEEEEEEK!

Every guest stopped what they were doing and stared. Both of the countess's eyes fell out in shock.

"Uh, hi, Mom . . . ," said Amelia as Countess Frivoleeta's left eyeball rolled across the floor after Squashy.

CHAPTER 20
GLITTEROPOLIS

Countess Frivoleeta stood frozen to the spot. Florence loomed over Tangine with one hairy fist raised.

"HE'S A CREATURE OF THE LIGHT! HE'S DANGEROUS!" she yelled.

"Florence, WAIT!" Amelia cried, picking herself up from the floor.

"There's a Creature of the Light in here?" shouted a cyclops from the crowd.

Tangine sat quietly as a sparkly tear slid down his face.

"GLIIIIIITTERRRRR!" a centaur shouted.

A monster started crying and the cyclops fainted, flattening a fat toad.

"Wait!" Amelia yelled. "Please! Stop! He's harmless!" But nobody was listening. Squashy bounced into Amelia's arms.

Count Drake was busy with a crossword in the corner of the room. "Everything okay over there, my dearest little snot-flicker?" he said without looking up.

An ogre roared and ran through the wall.

"Oh, good," the count said.

Most of the room had emptied, apart

from a few imps who
were stuck in puddles
of goblin slime.

"Florence," Amelia said, "please listen to
me and calm down. We have nothing to be
afraid of. Will you let me talk to Tangine?"

Florence looked confused but finally
stepped aside.

"Tangine," Amelia said softly. "Why didn't
you tell anyone about your mother?"

"Daddy told me not to," said Tangine, looking at the floor. "He said that Nocturnia would never accept a king who's half fairy."

"Surely it doesn't matter *what* you are, as long as you're a good king?" Amelia said gently. She sat down next to Tangine. "I saw a picture of your mom. She looked nice."

"I can't remember her much," Tangine said. "But I do remember she gave good hugs." He smiled a little. "Daddy spends every waking hour looking for her. I can't remember the last time he spent any real time with me."

"DIDN'T SHE TRY TO TAKE YOUR FANGS?" Florence bellowed.

"Didn't she blind you with fairy dust?" Grimaldi said curiously.

"No, none of that is true," said Tangine, frowning. "Those are just fairy tales."

"In the photos she looked very different

from the fairies we read about in class,"
Amelia said. "She had such a kind face."

"She was the loveliest creature I've
ever met," said a strong, deep voice.
King Vladimir looked around the room
and cleared his throat. "It's time I told the
truth.

"I met Fairyweather while I was out

playing in the Petrified Forest as a young vampire. I wasn't scared of her at all. She was just a sweet little fairy. From then on, we met every morning as the moon was setting and the sun was rising. And as the years went by, I fell in love. . . ."

Vladimir paused and closed his eyes for a moment.

"After Fairyweather disappeared, I felt empty," the king continued. "I dedicated my life to finding her. While searching the palace grounds, I saw something glimmering by the edge of the Petrified Forest. . . ."

"GLITTER?" said Florence.

"Of sorts," the king said. "It was the only clue I ever found. A small piece of rainbow parchment, with words written in glitter. It said, 'GLITTEROPOLIS, the city where the sun never goes down, and your dreams always come true . . .'

"I thought maybe Fairyweather had gone there, so I searched EVERYWHERE for Glitteropolis in the Kingdom of the Light. I lost sight of the family I still had—my son, who needed me." He bent down and put an arm around Tangine. "I'm sorry. I should have been there for you."

Tangine sighed and held his dad's hand. "It's OK, Daddy. I really want to find her too. The Mummy Maids are NOT good huggers. They're all . . . bumpy."

"Well," Amelia said, "maybe . . . maybe we could help?"

Grimaldi looked scared, but Tangine's eyes lit up. "You'd help me look for my mom?"

"Let's think of it as one epic game of hide-and-seek!" Amelia winked at Tangine.

"No goblin slime this time," he said with a shy smile.

"I can't promise anything." Amelia laughed and nudged his shoulder.

Florence stepped forward and puffed out her hairy chest. "I'M UP FOR A FAIRY HUNT—IN A NICE WAY, OF COURSE," she added. Then she coughed. "ER, SORRY FOR WANTING TO SQUISH YOU, PRINCE T."

Tangine smiled up at Florence. "Prince T . . ." He nodded. "I like that!"

Grimaldi stepped forward. "I'll help too!" he said, thumping his scythe on the ground. It finally stopped flashing. "Oh, thank darkness for that!"

Tangine looked up at the king and smiled. "Let's find Mom!"

King Vladimir beamed. "You're so like her, you know . . . well, when you're not being a spoiled sprout."

Amelia raised her eyebrows and Tangine frowned. They both started giggling. Tangine

paused, and then threw his arms around Amelia.

"Thhh-aaank you?" he said quietly. "Um, I don't think I've ever said that before."

Amelia chuckled. "You're welcome, Tangine."

Then he cleared his throat. "Squashy . . . sorry for, well, y'know."

Squashy looked at him with a little frown.

"Give him time," said Amelia. "You can make it up to him with some belly rubs!"

Amelia looked around at the ballroom. It was a complete disaster zone. She wandered over to her mom, who hadn't moved a muscle since her eyeballs had fallen out. "Um . . . sorry for ruining your ball, Mom," she said.

Count Drake sauntered over in his Hawaiian graveyard shirt and fluffy slippers. "You dropped your eyeballs, you silly snot-sausage." He smiled and picked them up, popping them back into Countess Frivoleeta's head.

The countess blinked and looked at Amelia.

Here we go, Amelia thought—*time for a big lecture on what a disappointment I am to the Fang family . . .*

"Ruined?" the countess said. A smile

began to crack across her face. "Darkling, that was the best Barbaric Ball we've had in years!" She fist-pumped the air and ripped the seam of her dress.

Amelia couldn't believe her ears. "You . . . you think so?" she said.

"Why," Countess Frivoleeta said, "it was positively disastrous. People will be talking about it for centuries!"

Amelia almost burst with happiness.

"OY! LOOK!" Florence was pointing at an imp dancing around Tangine's feet. The small puddle of goblin slime it had been stuck in was fizzling away.

"The glitter from Tangine's tears! It's dissolving the goblin slime! So THAT'S how you escaped my trap," she said to Tangine.

He smiled and shrugged.

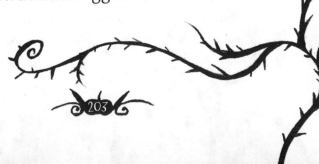

Amelia felt a wave of guilt. "I really am sorry about that. . . ."

"I suppose I deserved it. Bit of a lame trap, though," Tangine said with a smirk.

"Extraordinary," said Countess Frivoleeta, shuffling over. "I do believe we've found the solution to our goblin-slime problem!"

Squashy bobbed up and down in Amelia's arms.

"WELL, WHAT ARE WE WAITING

FOR?" Florence said. "WE'VE GOT A RESCUE MISSION TO PLAN!"

"You ready, Tangine?" Amelia said.

"BRENDA! FINNEGAN!" He clapped his hands twice.

"No, noooo," said Amelia, waving the Mummy Maids away again. "You won't be needing them."

"But who's going to do my hair?" asked Tangine.

"You are," Amelia said.

Tangine looked shocked. The king chuckled.

"I DUNNO ABOUT THE REST OF YOU, BUT I'M STARVING," said Florence, picking a piece of Jellied Brain off the floor.

Wooo flew into the almost-empty ballroom and stopped when he saw the mess.

"I'll get the mop," he said, and disappeared again.

The four new friends spent the rest of the night plotting how they were going to find Tangine's mom. As they made their plans, they used Grimaldi's scythe as a bat to sling Flabbergasting Fettuccine into Florence's hungry mouth. Tangine had surprisingly good aim, and Squashy bounced around gobbling up any leftovers.

Amelia laughed, digging in to some Toasted Earlobe Bites. "Y'know what?" she said as Squashy pa-doinged into her arms. "I can't believe I ever thought the Barbaric Ball was boring!"

THE END

Journey to the terrifying
Kingdom of the Light with Amelia
and her friends in book two!

Have you read all of Amelia's amazing adventures?

Available now!

About the Author

When she's not trying to take over the world or fighting sock-stealing monsters, Laura Ellen Anderson is a professional children's book author and illustrator, with an increasing addiction to coffee. She spends every waking hour creating and drawing, and would quite like to live on the moon when humans finally make it possible. Laura is the creator of *Evil Emperor Penguin* and illustrator of *Witch Wars*, as well as many other children's books. Amelia Fang is her first series as author-illustrator.

lauraellenanderson.co.uk
@laura_ellen_anderson
@Lillustrator